GU00985534

A Poisonous Plot

Lily Larkin Mysteries
Book 3

Hannah Ellis

Published by Hannah Ellis
www.authorhannahellis.com
Postfach 900309, 81503 München
Germany

Cover design by dmeacham design

A Poisonous Plot

Chapter One

It HAD BECOME a habit for Lily to unlock the door to the ice cream shop as soon as she went downstairs in the morning. The closed sign was enough to keep the general public out, and leaving the door unlocked meant anyone coming by for a social call could let themselves in. It saved Lily from trudging back and forth.

The dainty bell rang above the door just as she pulled her latest batch of ice cream from the freezer in the back room. Perhaps there would come a time when that sound annoyed the heck out of her, but the bell had only been installed a week ago and so far she loved it.

Her mouth watered even before she caught the scent of coffee, which drifted through at the same time that Flynn called "hello".

"I might end up like one of Pavlov's dogs," Lily said, stepping out from the back room and setting her tub of ice cream on the work surface behind the counter.

When he quirked an eyebrow in confusion, she kept talking.

"You know, the experiment with the dogs that had a conditioned response to a bell…" Surely he knew this.

"I know about the dogs," he said, handing over her coffee. "I'm only surprised you're admitting to salivating at the thought of seeing me."

"The coffee," she said, rolling her eyes. "The thought of *coffee* makes me salivate. Thank you," she added. "And good morning."

"Morning." In his police uniform, he always seemed to take up more space. That was probably the bulky stab vest, since his ego was big enough even when he was off duty.

"Hard at work, as always," she joked.

"It's a tough job keeping the Isles of Scilly free of crime," he replied mockingly. "I am actually here on official business, though." He leaned against the counter.

"What business?" She inhaled the delicious aroma of her coffee before taking a sip.

"You still haven't set a date for the grand opening of the ice cream shop. Which seems like a crime to me." He flashed a cocky grin, and she turned away from him to ease the lid from the ice cream tub and inspect the contents. She'd been happy with it when it had come out of the ice cream maker yesterday, but the flavours often changed subtly overnight.

"Lily?" Flynn growled impatiently. "What's the deal with the opening?"

She waved a dismissive hand. "I'm waiting for Rhys to finish the flyers and posters."

"It's difficult for him to do that without you giving him a date."

She turned and locked eyes with him. "You've been talking to Rhys about me?"

"I just saw him."

Lily glanced at her watch. "He'll have been out checking

the lobster pots with Ted, I suppose. Did he say if they've had much interest in the boat tours?"

He eyed her sternly. "Stop changing the subject. Choose a date and open the shop. Or don't set a date and just open."

"I'm not ready to open yet."

"You've spent a month doing the place up and perfecting your ice cream making techniques and flavours. You're ready to open."

"I'm waiting for a couple of pictures for the walls," she told him as her eyes swept the room.

The shop had been freshly painted, and the floor had been revamped with large black and white vinyl tiles. Alongside the original stainless-steel tables and chairs, the new flooring gave the place a wonderful retro vibe.

She had to admit, it looked fantastic. It also made her a little emotional to think about how much help she'd had from the community. So many people had pitched in.

"Also," she said in a rush. "I'm waiting for the health and safety inspection."

"You don't need to wait for that. You can open without it." Flynn sounded distinctly bored with the argument they'd been having for at least a week. "You've also taken more food hygiene courses than you need to. Just open the shop."

"I need to decide which ice cream flavours to start off with. I tried something new yesterday." She pointed at the tub in front of her.

"You can't change the subject that easily." His eyes lingered on the container and Lily knew it was exactly that easy to get him off topic. "What flavour is it?"

"Lemon curd and Biscoff."

He licked his lips.

"I made the lemon curd myself," she told him as she handed him a spoon.

"Fine. I'll test it." He ran the spoon through the ice cream, curling it into a neat scoop. "But we're still going to talk about..." He eyed the ice cream and his voice trailed off. "Whatever we were talking about," he muttered before shoving the spoon into his mouth.

Lily held her breath. "What do you think?"

"That's amazing." He groaned and slumped against the sideboard before reaching for another scoop.

She pushed his hand away. "Don't double dip!"

"You need to get me about fifty clean spoons then," he told her, tossing the spoon so it clattered into the sink.

"Or I could get you a bowl or a cone?"

"I'll take a cone and a lecture about eating ice cream for breakfast." His eyes flashed with amusement. "Or we could skip that today, if you'd like."

She took a cone from the container on top of the glass-fronted counter, then loaded it up for him. "I think I'll give up on lecturing you. You're a lost cause."

"My unhealthy breakfasts are entirely your fault, so the lectures are a little unfair." He licked around the edge of his ice cream. "This is seriously amazing."

The sound of the bell drew their attention, and they both smiled at the sight of the elderly lady striding in.

"Morning, Glynis," Flynn said.

"Ice cream for breakfast, PC Grainger?" She caught Lily's eye and shared a private smile. "Let's hope there are never any criminals who need chasing, because I'm not sure you'd be up to it."

"I'm perfectly fit!" Flynn said while he licked a stray blob of ice cream from the corner of his mouth. "Besides, don't pretend you're not about to eat ice cream at nine o'clock in the morning, too."

"I definitely didn't come here for intelligent conversation,"

Glynis remarked, then shuffled past the two of them to peer at the ice cream. "New flavour?"

Lily nodded. "Lemon curd and Biscoff."

"It's the best yet," Flynn said, right before his teeth crunched through his ice cream cone.

"Not better than the apple crumble?" Glynis craned her neck to look up at Flynn.

"Definitely better than that," he said firmly. "And better than the banana and hazelnut, and possibly even better than the cherry ripple chocolate..." He looked thoughtful. "That one's a close call. I'm undecided."

"Seriously?" Lily asked, her chest expanding as she inhaled a satisfied breath.

It was strange to think that a month ago she didn't have the slightest idea how to make ice cream, and even stranger to think that she might actually be good at it. To start with she'd just followed the recipes given to her by the shop's owner, but now she was experimenting with her own flavour combinations. She felt a rush of pride every time someone complimented her on her creations.

"I need to try this," Glynis said, helping herself to a cone.

She was in her eighties. Eighty-six to be exact. She'd announced it the first time they'd met, when she'd been passing on her morning walk and had called into the shop to introduce herself. Now, Lily saw her most mornings – sometimes she'd only wave as she power-walked along the promenade or sometimes she'd come in for a chat. Like Flynn, she was an enthusiastic taste-tester. A lot of the locals were. Lily was never short on people to give feedback on her flavours.

"Oh, that *is* good," Glynis remarked with a sigh. "It's up there with the apple crumble for me. So smooth and creamy, but then the crunch of the biscuit is perfect. The flavours are divine. The lemon really zings."

"Definitely time to open the shop and share your ice cream with the world," Flynn said pointedly.

"The world?" Lily asked, cocking her head.

"The island then." He popped the last of his cone into his mouth. "Though I reckon people will flock from far and wide to sample this."

"You know you'll get free ice cream without the flattery," Lily told him.

"Good to know." He brushed crumbs from his lips with the back of his hand. "I should go and see if I can find some crime to deal with. Wish me luck!"

Glynis clicked her tongue. "Most people find the lack of crime on these islands a positive thing."

"Not me," Flynn said. "Do me a favour, Glynis, and set up a crime ring of some sort. Give me something to do."

"Don't tempt me, PC Grainger. I have a lot of free time on my hands."

He snorted a laugh, then caught Lily's eye. "Pub tonight?"

She shrugged. "Okay."

"Let's try the Old Town Inn again. I'll pick you up after my shift."

The bell rang as he left.

"I don't know why he doesn't ask you out on a proper date," Glynis said through a mouthful of ice cream.

Lily wrinkled her nose. "What?"

"All these casual invitations to the pub. It's a ruse."

"He's helping me find the owner of this place," Lily said.

Admittedly, discreetly questioning residents in the local pubs hadn't got them anywhere yet, but since they'd decided going door to door was too intrusive, it at least felt as though she was doing something.

Glynis knew what their pub evenings were all about. As a long-time resident and self-proclaimed busybody Lily had hoped Glynis might have some information about the owner of the ice cream shop, but she hadn't been able to tell her anything other than the owner's name – Gail Greenway – which Lily had already known.

"You make a cute couple," Glynis said flatly.

"We're not a couple," Lily said, pressing hard on the lid of the ice cream to reseal it.

"You should be. He clearly fancies you." Mischief twinkled in Glynis's eyes. "I should get going too. Thank you for the ice cream. Enjoy your date tonight."

"It's not a date," Lily muttered. A complete waste of her breath.

Chapter Two

LILY WAS WAITING down in the shop when Flynn arrived early in the evening, dressed in jeans and a hoodie, which seemed to be his off-duty uniform.

"You didn't eat yet, did you?" he asked, stepping inside.

"No, I assumed we'd get dinner at the pub." It had become a bit of a routine. They'd take turns to pay.

"Good. I'm starving."

"You always are," Lily said, picking up her jacket and bag.

They both turned at a faint sound from outside. A tall, dark-haired man peered through the window. After raising his hand to wave, he pushed at the door, making the bell jingle. His white trainers squeaked on the vinyl floor, drawing Lily's gaze to his bright red socks which peeked out from his turned-up chinos. His navy polo shirt looked brand new. If you kept your eyes away from his feet, he looked like a stylish middle-aged guy.

"I need help," he said in a thick Italian accent. "There has been a crime and I need your help."

"What's happened?" Flynn asked, straightening up as his eyes flashed with something between hope and excitement.

"Not you." The man kept his eyes on Lily and extended his hand. "My name is Dante Accardi. It's nice to meet you. I need your help."

"Me?" Lily asked, glancing from Dante to Flynn. "This is PC Grainger..."

"Yes, I know. But I heard you are an investigator. I need an investigator. Police can't help me."

"If there's been a crime—" Flynn was cut off by Dante raising his hand and speaking over him.

"It's not police matter. I need investigator. You're new on this island, yes?"

"Yeah," Lily confirmed.

Dante's gaze roamed the room. "You help me and in return I'll tell you how to make gelato like we make in Italy. We have a deal?"

Lily's laughter came quickly, but stopped abruptly when Dante's sombre gaze bored into her.

"You're serious," she whispered.

"I'm serious. It's a good deal for you. Trust me."

"Why don't you tell me what the problem is and I'll see if I can help."

"Here's the thing," he said while drawing his phone out of his pocket. "I have a restaurant here. I moved here with my wife and daughter six months ago. We got settled in and I opened my restaurant one month ago. The first two weeks, everything is good. People love my food. My food is fantastic. I not lie." He gesticulated wildly and Lily made sure not to catch Flynn's eye for fear that she might get the giggles.

"Before I live here," he went on. "I lived for fifteen years in London. I had my own restaurant, everything was great. But London is too busy for me. I wanted to go back to Italy and find a quiet village where life is not all rushing and busy. You know?"

Lily nodded her acknowledgement.

"My wife is British. Not speak good Italian. She won't move to Italy. So we do the... what's the word ... compromise. We compromise! We move here. This is the place where my wife came for childhood holidays. So we came here. Nice people, not so busy. Happy Dante!" He patted his chest as he paused. "Then terrible thing happen," he said, lowering his voice and shaking his head. "This is not nice to see, Lily, but I must show you..." As he tapped on his phone, Lily braved a glance at Flynn, whose eyebrows had drawn close together.

"If it's disturbing images..." Flynn said.

"It is disturbing all right," Dante said, thrusting the phone at Lily. "But not images, words. Disturbing words. Read this. I can't look."

Lily took the phone from him. "It's reviews," she said as she scanned the screen. "Reviews for your restaurant?" She shifted slightly so Flynn could see the screen.

"Yes. These reviews say my food is bad, that it makes people sick." Dante shook his head furiously. "This is crazy. I am a top chef. I make wonderful food. No one gets sick. Then I come here to these Scilly Islands. Open my restaurant. Two weeks everything is good and then this..." He jabbed a finger towards the phone.

Lily winced as she read through the dozen or so reviews where people complained of varying degrees of upset stomachs after eating in his restaurant.

"I'm not sure how I can help," Lily said when Dante stared at her. "What makes you think a crime has been committed? There's nothing illegal about the reviews. They look as though they're from legitimate accounts."

"I'll show you the problem." Dante took the phone back and scrolled for a moment. "This review," he announced after a moment. "This one is where problem starts..."

Lily read the five-star review aloud. *"Great food and atmosphere and the owner is a lovely, friendly man. A lot of foreigners keep arriving to take island jobs though."* She glanced at Flynn. "That's weird."

"That's when the problem started," Dante said.

"But his review of the restaurant is really good," Lily pointed out. "It's confusing. It also doesn't make a lot of sense since you haven't taken a job from anyone. Aren't you providing employment by opening a restaurant?"

"My wife and daughter work for me." He shook his head. "But I might employ more people if I had more customers."

"It's a weird review anyway," Lily said.

"Some weird people. Many, many weird people. But I tell you this is when the problems started. You need to find this person."

Lily read the name of the reviewer. "The Secret B."

"This is the big problem with the internet," Dante said loudly. "People hide behind false names. But you are an investigator. You can find him. Bring him to me and I will take care of things from there. In return, I teach you about gelato."

Lily's brain struggled to keep up with the conversation. "You really think this person has set up some kind of hate campaign against you? He's writing fake reviews to run you out of business?"

Dante shook his head and stared at her as though she'd missed the point entirely.

"These are real reviews," he said as a deep frown furrowed his brow. "People really got ill. I know because I got ill too."

"Maybe it was a stomach bug," Lily suggested. "It might not have been down to the food."

"It's the food," Dante said with certainty.

"I'm sorry, I'm a bit lost."

"This man..." He jabbed at the phone. "This man poisoned my customers. You find him for me and I'll deal with him the way we deal with things in Italy. Okay?"

"That's definitely not okay," Flynn said.

Dante's eyes jerked to Flynn as though only just remembering he was there. "This not a police matter. Not concern you."

"It will concern me if you go all vigilante and decide you're the Italian mafia of the island. You can't take the law into your own hands."

"Vigilante! What are you talking about? I said I deal with problem like in Italy. In Italy we deal with problems man to man. We sit down and talk and drink and eat... and we keep talking until we understand each other." He clicked his tongue. "*Italian mafia!* You watch too many films." With a shake of his head, he dismissed Flynn and retrieved his phone from Lily. "I'll give you a few days. In this time I must close the restaurant and do big cleaning and try and fix this mess."

"Wait," Lily said as he strode across the room. "How on earth would he have poisoned them? Surely you'd have noticed someone slipping into the restaurant every evening to poison the food."

"I don't know how he did it," Dante said dramatically. "Maybe he did something to the water or put something in the air or tampered with something else. When you find him, you bring him to me and I'll ask him what he did. Then we'll know and we can fix everything. I rely on you, Lily."

"Hang on," she said desperately, but he was already gone.

Flynn flashed her a smug grin. "You get all the fun cases."

"This is not a case," Lily said. "Clearly, the man is a bad cook. Or he bought some dodgy ingredients or something."

"That's for you to figure out," Flynn said.

Lily gave his arm a friendly shove and glared at him.

"You could also go to the restaurant and tell him you don't accept the case, but you may end up ill."

"I also don't think he'll take no for an answer."

"Are you actually going to look into it?"

Lily pulled her bag onto her shoulder and shook her head. "I'll just tell him I couldn't find anything when he comes back. Now, are we going for dinner or what?"

Chapter Three

WHILE HE WAITED for the barman to pour their drinks at the Old Town Inn, Flynn glanced across at Lily, sitting at the small round table at the side of the room. Her shoulder-length, chestnut hair cast her face in shadow as she peered at her phone.

Spending time with her made island life much more bearable. He only wished he could be more helpful in figuring out who owned the ice cream shop. It was clear how much the subject bothered her, and that, in turn, bothered him.

"Food shouldn't be too long," the wiry barman told him as he set the drinks on the bar.

"Thanks," Flynn said, before crossing the room to return to their table. "You look very intense," he told Lily when she didn't look up from her phone.

"It's weird," she said, her thumb trailing over the screen. "He really *did* have a successful restaurant. He had awards and everything."

Flynn took a long sip of his pint. "Who?"

"Dante. The Italian guy. I looked him up."

"I thought you weren't going to look into that."

"I wasn't." Her eyes sparkled when she lifted her gaze. "You know me, though."

"I do. What did you find?"

"He had a thriving Italian restaurant in central London. The reviews are fantastic."

"So it's not that he's bad at his profession."

"Definitely not."

"Surely someone isn't really trying to sabotage his business?"

"I wouldn't have thought so." Lily reached for her drink, but only tapped her nails against the side of the glass. "I suppose I can see why he'd think that. Putting myself in his shoes, I can't imagine how horrible it must feel to get the reviews he's been getting. If I got reviews like that for the ice cream shop..." She puffed her cheeks out and didn't bother to finish the sentence.

Flynn shook his head. "You're not going to poison anyone. Please don't start coming up with more reasons to put off opening."

"I'm not. As soon as I have my menu finalised and everything else finished, I'll open."

He could see the doubt in her eyes and wished there was something he could do to reassure her. Her nerves around the opening didn't even make sense. The shop looked fantastic and the ice cream really was delicious.

"It's going to be great." He took another sip of his pint. "You know that, right?"

She glanced around the room, but didn't seem to take anything in. "I don't even know why I'm so nervous about it," she said quietly. "If it doesn't work out, I won't really have lost anything. It's not as though my life will fall apart if the ice cream shop isn't successful."

Financially, it wouldn't be a big deal. At least that was the impression she gave. He wasn't entirely sure of Lily's situation but knew that she'd inherited enough money that finances weren't something she worried about.

"Just because you don't need the place to be a financial success doesn't mean you don't have your heart set on it doing well."

She nodded, but didn't meet his gaze. "I guess that's it. I want to do well at something for once."

"I've only ever seen you succeed," he said flatly.

He genuinely couldn't imagine Lily failing at anything. Even if things didn't go her way, she'd pick herself up and keep going.

"I have something to show you," he said, changing the subject. Reaching into his pocket, he pulled out a glossy photograph.

"What's that?" Lily took it from him and stared at it in awe.

"The original photo of the owner," he explained. "It's not much better than the version you found online, but it's not cropped. I think it's a little clearer."

"It is," she said, then squinted. "It's still difficult to make out her features properly. And I still don't recognise her." She sucked in a breath. "How did you get this?"

"Emailed a few people," he said casually, not wanting to admit it was a lot of people. "I may have implied I was asking as a matter of official police business."

"Thank you," she said, her smile making all the emails worthwhile.

"I'm not sure how helpful it will be."

"I appreciate the effort," she said, but clearly she also didn't think it would help.

"We'll figure it out, eventually."

"How?" Lily asked. "Gail Greenway clearly doesn't want to be found and no one we ask has any information about her. If she's living on the island, someone would have seen her."

"Yes, but it's also plausible that people wouldn't recognise her after twenty years. She might look completely different now."

Lily gazed down at the photo. "I don't think I want to keep looking for her."

"Really?"

"I want to know because I'm nosey." Her features softened slightly. "And because I can't seem to stop wondering. But I also can't help but think..." She paused and chewed her lip.

"What?" Flynn asked impatiently.

"If the owner was somehow connected to my parents – if she knew them – and she knew me when I was a kid... she doesn't want to know me now. So while it would be satisfying to figure out who she is, I suspect it would also be really unsatisfying in another way."

Flynn stretched his leg out under the table so his leg rested against hers. "She wanted you to have the shop," he pointed out.

Lily smiled sadly as she shrugged. "It doesn't make sense. And I want it to make sense, but I think it might drive me crazy trying to figure it out."

"Do you know what might help?" Flynn said, feeling the warmth of her leg against his.

"What?" she asked, with a hint of an eye roll.

"You should open the shop. Being busier will help take your mind off it." He sat up straighter and immediately regretted it when his leg was no longer touching hers. "You could put the photo of the owner up on the wall, and frame the article about the fire... you never know, that might get people talking. Someone might remember something helpful."

"Maybe," Lily said, but he suspected her smile was all for his benefit. She just didn't like to thwart his enthusiasm. "Tell me about your day," she said, in that relaxed way of hers.

He smiled in response because they really had this routine perfected now. She asked about work, and he regaled her with overly dramatic stories about rural policing. It was a test of his imagination to put a humorous spin on his uneventful days, but it had the effect of making his working days easier since he often found himself conjuring entertaining interpretations of the most mundane tasks ready for when he spoke to Lily.

He had an anecdote about a dispute over a property border ready for her, but he didn't even get a word out before they were interrupted.

"Hi, Ted," Lily said, glancing up as the lobster fisherman wandered over to them. They'd got to know him well when his stepson had gone missing, and he'd subsequently been helpful with renovating Lily's new place.

"I was just thinking about you," he told Lily. "Do you have a date for opening the shop yet?"

"We were just discussing it," Flynn replied for her. "We were thinking of the weekend after next. Saturday would be good, I think."

"Perfect." Ted grinned. "I'll get Rhys to finish the posters, and we can start spreading the word."

"I didn't agree to that," Lily snapped at Flynn. "I need to wait and make sure I'm prepared for the hygiene inspection."

"No, you don't. Besides, that could be months away." Flynn caught Ted's eye. "Tell Rhys to go ahead with the posters. If he emails them to me, I'll organise getting them printed."

He could feel Lily glaring at him.

"I can organise getting them printed," she said.

"I'm sure you *can*," Flynn agreed. "I'm just not sure you *will*."

"Are you nervous?" Ted asked Lily. "There's no need – not given how delicious your ice cream is."

Flynn nodded. "This is what I keep telling her."

"I'll make sure I keep the day free so I can help if you need me to..." Ted trailed off as his gaze snagged on the photograph on the table. "Is that another photo of the owner of the ice cream shop?"

"It's just a slightly better version of the picture we already have." Lily seemed to hold her breath while Ted picked the photo up to scrutinise it. "What is it?" she finally asked, an edge to her voice that had Ted looking as though he'd been snapped out of a trance.

"Nothing," he said apologetically. "I was only thinking that it looks as though she didn't want to have her photo taken. The way she has her head tilted so her face is in shadow."

"Yeah." Lily took the photo back. "It would be helpful if we had a clear photo of her. And a recent one."

Ted gave her a sympathetic smile. "Anyway, should I tell Rhys to finish up the posters? Is it a definite for two weeks from now?"

"It's a definite," Flynn said, before Lily could protest.

Ted stepped out of the way when the waitress appeared with their dinner, then told them to enjoy their food and left them alone.

"I didn't agree to opening on the Saturday," Lily said sulkily, once the waitress had moved away.

"I'll be there with you," he said. "You've got nothing to worry about. If anything, you should be excited."

She blew out a breath. "You're right."

24

"Of course I am," he quipped, then shifted his leg out of the way when she went to kick him.

"I should be excited," she agreed reluctantly. "I hate that I'm stressing about this. I'll open in two weeks." She took a deep breath. "That means I have some work to do."

Chapter Four

The Pengelly Garden Centre was located to the north of the airport. As well as selling plants, garden furniture and a selection of gifts and cards, it also boasted a cafe and a farm shop with a selection of fruits, vegetables and herbs. When Lily had met the owner, Gordon Pengelly, on one of her previous visits, he'd told her the business had started as his own private vegetable garden which had got out of hand.

The produce was great quality and Lily had been utilising it for her ice cream experiments. She'd continue to do so when the shop opened, and intended to have a seasonal menu, alongside the staples of vanilla and chocolate.

As part of her push to get ready for opening the shop, she was meeting with Gordon to get a list of the fruits and herbs he could supply her with over the next few months. She'd finalise the menu based on that.

It still felt a little daunting. She knew Flynn was right that she should stop panicking about it and open the shop, but the thought of it made her insides twist. That was probably mostly imposter syndrome. She felt in no way qualified to open an ice cream shop, even though the feedback on her flavours couldn't be better.

"I think that's everything I can offer," Gordon told her, leaning back in his chair, across from Lily. His office at the back of the garden centre was spacious and, judging by the number of people who'd come and gone while they chatted, he seemed to have an open-door policy.

Lily glanced down at her notes. "I'll go through all this and decide on the menu. Then I can let you know what I'll need." She smiled uncertainly, reminding herself that she was on a steep learning curve and everything would get easier. "I guess I won't know the exact quantities I'll need to start with, but you said you can be flexible."

"Of course." He smiled and interlaced his fingers across his round belly. "Not a problem."

A female voice interrupted them. "It's great that you're going with seasonal produce for your flavours."

Lily's gaze snapped up to Gordon's daughter, Sally. She'd been in and out of the office a few times and wasn't shy about offering her opinions on Lily's business venture. Not that Lily minded, especially as she seemed to have a head for business.

"It will keep things interesting for the locals too," Sally went on, idly curling her long blonde hair around her finger as she spoke. "Never knowing what will be on the menu. You'll get people coming in purely out of curiosity."

Lily shifted in the uncomfortable wooden chair. "I was going to stick to the same menu for a few months. I'll change the menu with the seasons."

"Oh." Sally frowned and leaned against the desk. "I assumed you'd change the menu from one week to the next, depending on what ingredients are available, or even from day to day during the busy season."

"I'd have to keep printing the menu, so it wouldn't be great from an environmental perspective."

"I assumed you'd just have a blackboard," Sally said blithely. "But of course if you have printed menus it wouldn't make sense."

Lily's stomach tightened. Why hadn't she thought of having a blackboard? That made way more sense. Apparently, she'd been too caught up in perfecting the ice cream to really consider the basic setup of the shop.

"It's a good idea," she said, nodding.

"It would also work better for us. Then you could take more of the stock we need to get rid of. For example, berries which are only available for a limited period."

Lily continued to nod. "That's a good idea. I'm also happy to be flexible about what I take from you."

"Great." Sally moved past the desk and patted her dad on the shoulder. "It sounds as though it will be a really positive working relationship."

He squeezed her hand. "Sally has good business instincts," he told Lily.

"You must be very happy to have her around."

"I am," he said with a pointed look at his daughter. "I'm sure the place would go to pot without her."

Sally rolled her eyes. "You managed fine while I was away at sixth form, and then university." She cast her gaze to Lily. "He's not happy with me because I'm moving back to the mainland at the end of the summer."

"More studying?" Lily asked.

"No. I just graduated. It's finally time to start my career. If I can find a job, anyway."

"I don't know why you can't find something on the islands," Gordon grumbled.

"Because there are very limited career options here," Sally told him. "As you well know. How many more times are we going to have this conversation?" She smiled at him affectionately.

"What area do you want to work in?" Lily asked.

"I studied accounting, which I know sounds very boring, but I've always loved numbers. My plan is to set up an accounting firm one day, but I'll work for someone else for a while to gain experience."

Lily smiled politely and slipped her notepad into her bag.

"How's the green smoothie going down?" Sally asked, tipping her chin toward the drink in front of Lily.

"It's good." Reaching for it, she stifled a grimace at the thought of drinking any more. She should have trusted her instincts and gone for a coffee, but when Gordon had recommended the green smoothie the healthy option had felt like a good idea.

"It's surprisingly filling," she said, forcing another mouthful down. There was no way she could manage any more of the thick gloop that tasted of grass.

"Think of the health benefits," Sally said. "It's the only way I can get them down."

"It tastes fine," she lied, not wanting to offend her new business partner.

Sally gave her an indulgent look. "I can put it in a take-away cup if you want?"

"That would be perfect," Lily said, a rush of gratitude making her want to claim Sally as her new best friend.

"Have you set a date for the opening of the ice cream shop?" Gordon asked, standing when Lily did.

"Two weeks." She assumed Flynn and Ted wouldn't let her wriggle out of it so she may as well bite the bullet. "On the Saturday."

"That's exciting," Sally said as she reached for the smoothie. "I'll definitely come along on opening day. I'm desperate to try these flavour combinations you've been talking about. They sound divine."

"Just call ahead to confirm your first order," Gordon said. "Then I can have everything ready for you."

"Thank you."

Gordon offered his hand. "I'm looking forward to working with you."

"You too," Lily said. Hopefully, at some point it would sink in that this was her life now, and the idea of running an ice cream shop would feel normal. "I'll be in touch again soon."

"I'll look forward to it," Gordon said and stayed behind in his office.

The little cafe area at the back of the garden centre was manned by Arthur, a tall, smiley man who Lily had been introduced to when she arrived. He was one of those people whose age was hard to judge. At a guess, she'd say he was probably in his thirties, but his tweed jacket and green wellies gave him the air of someone older, as did his grey corduroy trousers, which were cinched at the waistband by a brown belt.

He stood aside when Sally moved behind him to get a takeaway cup. "Can I get you anything else?" he asked Lily.

"No, I'm fine, thank you."

His smile remained wide as his eyes lingered on Lily. "I'm an expert on houseplants if you ever need advice or a recommendation."

"Thank you," Lily said politely.

"Not just houseplants." Sally handed the smoothie over in a takeaway cup. "Arthur is an expert in all kinds of plants.

Some might say he's a little obsessed." She flashed him a teasing grin that was full of affection.

"I have other hobbies too," he said proudly. "I like art."

"But not as much as plants," Sally said with a smile.

"I'm a qualified botanist," he said, eyes locked on Lily.

"That's great."

"Do you know a lot about plants?" he asked.

"I'm afraid not, but I'm learning a lot about which herbs I can use in ice cream flavours."

"You're opening the ice cream shop on the promenade," he said with a nod. "That's exciting."

"It is," she agreed and took a step away.

"If you want, I can show you around here and teach you about the plants."

"I think Lily needs to get back to making plans for the ice cream shop," Sally said, giving Arthur a pat on his back.

"I do actually," Lily said, grateful to Sally once again. "I'm sure I'll see you both again soon."

She made a quick getaway, walking briskly through the indoor section of the garden centre. Outside, she almost crashed into a guy pushing a wheelbarrow with a huge plant in it – some kind of exotic-looking palm tree. She'd also met him when she arrived. He was a freelance landscape gardener who also did some work around the garden centre.

"Sorry," she said, stopping just in front of him.

"No worries. Lily, was it?"

"Yes." She tried to recall his name but came up blank. "Sorry. I have a memory like a sieve sometimes..."

"Denzel." Laughter lines crinkled around his eyes when he smiled. He was probably in his fifties and had the solid build of a man who made his living from manual labour. "Have you got all of your ice cream flavours sorted?"

"I think so."

"Glad to hear it. I've always had a thing for banana ice cream." He winked at her and set off again. "Just in case you're taking requests."

"I'll bear it in mind." She watched him continue on his way, before ambling along and letting her gaze roam over the rows of plants.

When rays of sunshine escaped from behind a fluffy white cloud, she lifted her face to bask in the tingling warmth on her cheeks. Spring would turn to summer soon. A great time to open an ice cream shop, she told herself firmly.

Maybe she should have taken Arthur up on his offer of a tour, because her knowledge of plants really was quite pathetic. There was something soothing about wandering through them, and instead of heading straight for the exit, she meandered and checked out the selection of garden ornaments and then wandered slowly along a row bursting with brightly coloured perennials.

Stopping, her eyes followed a pair of white butterflies and she only looked up again when she caught sight of someone waving in her peripheral vision.

"Hi!" Lily said as Glynis tramped towards her in a pair of hiking boots, looking far younger and fitter than most people her age.

"Beautiful day, isn't it? I walked all the way here."

"You're amazingly active," Lily said.

"I need to be. It's sitting around and doing nothing that makes people frail. I'm avoiding frailty at all costs."

"You're doing a good job of it." Lily followed Glynis's gaze as she glanced behind her.

"I'm here with a friend," Glynis said. "You should meet her. I keep telling her all about your ice cream." She lifted her hand and waved manically. "Maria," she called.

The woman looked up from the plants she was peering at.

"Come here!" Glynis crooned. "I want you to meet someone. This is Lily, who I keep telling you about..."

The woman's smile fell away, and she glanced towards the building as though she might bolt.

"She's very shy," Glynis explained, taking Lily's arm and steering her towards her friend. "Lovely though, once you get to know her."

"Hi," the woman said, holding out a limp hand to Lily. "I'm Maria."

"Maria's my carer," Glynis put in.

"You have a carer?" Lily blurted out, then grimaced when she realised how shocked she sounded. "Sorry. I'm just surprised you need a carer."

"I'm more like a lodger," Maria said.

"Nonsense. She's a big help around the house. And it gives me peace of mind to have someone around. There's a great comfort in knowing I'll be found promptly if I die in my sleep. I hate the thought of rotting away until the neighbours notice the smell."

"Don't be so grim," Maria admonished.

Glynis only shrugged. "Twenty years from now, you'll be having the same concerns."

"If I make it that long," the woman said. "You'll probably outlive me." Her eyes strayed to Lily, then quickly away again. "I should go in and see if I can find what I need for the window boxes."

"You could also ask if they're looking for any staff," Glynis said. "I think you'd enjoy working in the cafe a few mornings a week."

"Don't nag," Maria said gently before wandering away.

Glynis waited until she was out of hearing before speaking again. "I've told her she needs something to get her out of the house. I think a part-time job would be perfect for her, but she doesn't seem keen on the idea."

"Have you known her long?" Lily asked.

"We've been friends for a long time, but she just moved in with me a few months ago." Her eyes went to her retreating friend. "She was living in Bristol. Retired not too long ago, and she's been living alone since she got divorced. I've been nagging her to visit me for years. When she finally agreed, I persuaded her to come for an extended stay. I thought the change would be good for her, but I worry that she doesn't socialise much."

"A job sounds like a good idea," Lily remarked. "And working in a garden centre sounds nice. The cafe's cute." She lifted the drink in her hand. "I don't recommend the green smoothie, though."

"Don't say that!" Glynis beamed. "It's my drink of choice." She patted her stomach. "It may not be the tastiest treat, but it keeps me regular."

"That might be a bit too much information," Lily said, making Glynis laugh loudly. "It's definitely not to my taste," she went on. "If you don't mind the fact that I've had two sips, you're welcome to it. Otherwise, it'll go in the bin when I get home."

"Don't mind if I do," Glynis said, taking it from her. "That'll save me a few quid." She sucked at the straw and grimaced. "It's worse than usual. Very bitter today. It'll keep me full of energy, that's the main thing. By the way, how was your evening in the pub with your sexy policeman?"

Lily heaved in an exasperated breath as she shook her head. "I had a nice evening with Flynn."

"You won't even admit he's lovely to look at?"

"He's my friend. That's all."

"Not denying it either." Glynis patted Lily's cheek like an affectionate grandmother. "I'll see you tomorrow for my morning ice cream fix if there's some going."

"There will always be ice cream waiting for you," Lily said, then laughed when Glynis took another sip of the smoothie and grimaced dramatically.

Chapter Five

WITH THE VISIT to the garden centre out of the way, Lily spent the afternoon deciding on the ice cream flavours she'd offer for the shop opening. Once she had the menu finalised, she could call Gordon to give him her shopping list. She'd also need to put in an order with the supermarket to make sure she had enough cream and the other products which she couldn't get from the garden centre.

It should have been a straightforward task, but after questioning her decisions, she decided to sleep on it and put in her orders the following day. She did order blackboard paint for the back wall of the shop, along with chalk pens, so she felt sufficiently productive.

By the time she crawled into bed, she was feeling more positive about the opening of the shop. Deep down, she knew that she just needed to swallow her nerves and get on with it.

Sadly, any positive feelings had left her when she woke in the middle of the night. In their place were pangs of nausea and intense stomach cramps. It felt as though her insides were being squeezed, and she instinctively rolled onto her side and brought her knees towards her chest. The motion didn't help, and she spent half an hour writing on her bed before forcing herself up to get a glass of water.

Moving helped a little, and she wandered the flat, wondering if the nausea which came in waves would get strong enough for her to vomit, and if she'd feel better if she did.

When the pain faded, she slipped back into bed and dozed for an hour or two before waking to an overpowering rush of nausea. Springing from the bed, she just made it to the bathroom in time to rid herself of the contents of her stomach.

The relief was immediate and she rinsed her mouth out before trudging back to bed and falling straight into a deep sleep.

When she woke again in the middle of the morning, a dull ache had replaced the cramps, as though someone had punched her repeatedly in the stomach. An unhealthy dose of self-pity accompanied the discomfort. Being ill was never pleasant, but being ill alone was miserable.

She thought of how her uncle had coddled her when she was ill as a kid, and missed him so fiercely it brought tears to her eyes.

A distraction was what she needed, she told herself as she dragged her duvet to the couch and switched the TV on. It didn't help, and ten minutes later she had her phone in her hand, typing out a message to Flynn, casually asking how work was going.

Thrilling as ever, he replied, and she smiled at the words which she knew were all sarcasm. *I've made the sergeant two cups of tea this morning, cleared up the front desk, washed the Land Rover and shooed a cat out of the station three times. Crime fighting at its most intense.*

Lily's smile stretched wider and she didn't have a chance to respond before he messaged again.

How's everything in the ice cream world? Any new flavours I need to test?

Not today, she told him. *I'm ill.*

All she got back was a couple of question marks.

Was up half the night with stomach cramps and vomiting, she wrote.

A sad face emoji came through. *How are you feeling now?*

A bit pathetic, but physically much better.

Do you need me to bring you anything?

No, I'm okay, thanks. Just lazing on the couch and feeling sorry for myself.

I can call over later if the sergeant feels capable of dealing with the stray cat alone.

She chuckled and it made her stomach hurt. *I might be contagious,* she typed.

I'll take my chances. Let me know if you think of anything you need. I can call at the shop.

Thank you, she typed, then flopped back onto the couch, feeling infinitely better.

It was an hour later when she heard from him again, messaging to say he was downstairs and she should throw her keys down. That was definitely better than trudging all the way down there in her pyjamas.

"How are you feeling?" he asked when he wandered in wearing his uniform and holding a shopping bag in his hand.

"Okay." She kept her head on the cushion and couldn't even muster the energy to sit up. "My stomach feels as though someone used it as a punchbag, but other than that, I'm all right."

He held up the shopping bag. "I brought you chamomile

tea, a couple of tins of soup and a hot water bottle. I assumed you probably wouldn't have one."

Warmth spread through her chest, and it took her a moment to find her voice. "Thank you," she murmured.

"I'll make you a tea. Are you hungry?"

"I don't know," she said weakly.

"If you're not up to soup, I also brought bread. I can make you a slice of toast and see how it goes down."

"That would be good." She was glad he immediately went to the kitchen, so she had a moment to get her emotions under control.

They were friends and she'd absolutely do the same for him, so she shouldn't be surprised by him looking after her. Really, that was why she'd messaged him. She'd wanted someone to take care of her, but she'd only expected a bit of sympathy.

"Is it okay for you to go shopping while on duty?" she asked when he came back with a cup of tea and the hot water bottle.

He placed the steaming mug on the coffee table and raised an eyebrow. "I spent a good portion of the morning chasing a cat out of the station and had a half hour meeting with the sergeant about whether we should just let the cat have free rein of the place. I don't think you need to worry about me wasting taxpayers' money. This is probably the most useful thing I'll do all day." He perched on the couch beside her thigh. "You know what I was thinking while I was in the supermarket?"

"What?"

"I kept glancing around, hoping I might catch someone shoplifting. Someone in good physical shape who'd give me a run for my money while I chased them down. I miss the feeling of tackling shoplifters to the ground. That's sad, isn't it?"

"A bit," she agreed at the same time that the toaster popped in the kitchen.

Flynn handed over the hot water bottle. "Put that against your stomach. When I was a kid my mum used to give me a hot water bottle when I was ill and it was always very soothing."

She pushed it under her blanket and held it against her stomach.

"Sorry, I can't stay longer," Flynn said when he returned from the kitchen with a single slice of toast.

"Don't be daft. You have to get to work. I really appreciate you coming over at all."

"Message me later and let me know how you're feeling. There's soup in the kitchen if you feel up to it later."

"Thank you. I hope work is busier for you this afternoon."

He arched an eyebrow. "I'm going to have a busy afternoon making a bed for a stray cat."

"That sounds like fun," she said, her lips curving into a smile.

"You have a weird idea of fun." He gave a quick wave before leaving her alone.

The visit perked her up, as did the tea and toast. Watching a film while snuggling with a hot water bottle felt lovely and indulgent now. By the time the credits rolled up at the end, she felt her appetite returning and was lured by the thought of a nice, warm bowl of soup.

In the kitchen, she stopped in front of the table. When she'd moved in, Mirren Treneary had given her a pretty white vase as a housewarming gift, but it had never been used. Not until now, when cheerful giant daisies rose out of it.

Beside it was a note in Flynn's messy handwriting which simply said *Get well soon.* She lowered her face and inhaled the faint scent of the flowers, then moved to warm up the soup.

It was a shame he was such a womaniser. He'd make someone a great boyfriend if he felt so inclined.

Chapter Six

AFTER ANOTHER DAY OF REST, Lily felt completely normal again. Flynn messaged her in the morning to ask if she was feeling up to a run, but she declined. She might feel normal but she wasn't feeling overly energetic. Besides, now that she was feeling better she had to face the reality that she'd be opening the shop soon. She needed to prepare.

As had become her habit, she went down to the shop to tackle anything work related. First on the agenda was finalising the menu for opening day so she could put in an order for the ingredients she'd need and get to work building up a supply of ice cream.

She was scribbling away in her notebook when Flynn wandered in in the middle of the morning. Given his jeans and T-shirt and his fresh appearance, she gathered he hadn't come straight from his workout.

"How was your run?" she asked.

"Good." He glanced through the window. "Beautiful blue skies this morning. You missed out. How are you feeling now?"

"Fine. Just not quite up to a run. Besides, I decided I

better get to work if you're going to insist on bullying me into opening in a week and a half."

"I am." He dropped a stack of papers in front of her and pulled out a chair. "I've just printed these out. What do you think?"

"They're great," she said, picking up a flyer and forcing a smile. Rhys had done a brilliant job creating a simple, but effective design – with all the information about the opening of the ice cream shop, along with some cute graphics. "Thank you."

"You're really worried about this, aren't you?" Flynn said softly.

"No." She shook her head but wasn't fooling herself, so knew there was no way she was fooling Flynn. "Okay, I am," she amended. "And I know it's stupid, but I can't help it."

"It's not stupid. Of course it's nerve wracking, but it's exciting too, isn't it?"

"It should be, but I guess I've been too busy worrying about it to be excited." She set the flyer down. "I've always worked for someone else, and I don't think I ever did anything that required me to take a lot of pride in my work. I really want this to do well." She sighed heavily. "What if I open and no customers turn up? Or if they hate the ice cream and never come back?"

"That's not going to happen," Flynn said with absolute certainty. "The shop will be a success. You're too stubborn for it not to be."

That drew a smile from her. "You may have a point there. Though I think you mean I'm determined, not stubborn."

His mouth twitched at the corners. "Sure. If that's what you want to call it. Anyway, are we going to plaster this island with flyers, or what?"

"Now?"

"I don't see why not. The weather is gorgeous."

"Okay." She nodded, but her eyes flicked to the door.

"Do you have other plans?" Flynn asked.

"No." She tapped on the table. "I just thought Glynis might stop by. I haven't seen her the last two days. She specifically told me she was going to call in."

Flynn looked at his watch. "She's usually here earlier than this, isn't she?"

"Yeah. I guess she isn't coming today. We should go and put the posters up." Since Flynn had gone to so much effort, it would be rude not to. Also, she needed to stop letting fear rule her. She'd put the flyers up and open the shop. Everything would be fine. She sucked in a deep breath. "First, I need to get your opinion on the menu for opening day."

With his usual level-headed approach, he went through it all with her, then waited while she called the garden centre to put in an order for herbs and berries. Then she called the supermarket and gave them her order for cream, sugar and other ingredients.

It was almost midday when they set off for their walk around the island, pinning and taping flyers as they went. Several people stopped to see what they were doing and just about everyone enthusiastically said they'd come along to the opening.

"What if I don't have enough ice cream?" Lily said as they made their way towards the Mermaid Inn – the last stop on their tour.

"What?" Flynn asked.

"What if too many people turn up on opening day and I don't have enough stock?"

"Make a lot of stock," he said, opening the door and holding it for her. "Given how little there is to do around here, I imagine you'll get most of the islanders calling in."

"Don't say that!" She glared at him as she stepped inside. "If everyone comes, I definitely won't have enough ice cream."

"Okay, not everyone will come, but you have a lot of freezer space. Just make more than you think you'll need. Better to have too much than too little."

She shook her head as they headed for the bar. "Earlier I was panicking that no one would come. Now I'm worrying about the opposite. I would never have thought opening an ice cream shop would be this stressful."

"I'll be there with you," he said, resting an elbow on the bar. "Everything will go perfectly, but if there are any problems, I promise to cause some kind of distraction so no one notices."

"Like what?" Lily asked, amused.

He looked thoughtful. "If you run out of ice cream, I'll claim there are too many people in the shop. I'll spout something about legal capacity and kick everyone out."

Lily's eyes widened. "Is there a law about how many people I can have in the shop at one time?"

"Oh, my god!" Flynn laughed loudly. "I need to stop opening my mouth because it feels like anything I say is going to stress you out."

"Who's stressed?" Seren asked, appearing from the kitchen with a plate of food in each hand.

"Guess?" Lily said. "It seems like an easy one though... have you ever known Flynn to get stressed?"

"Good point." Seren moved out from behind the bar. "I'll be right back."

They watched as she delivered food to a table nearby, then returned to the bar.

"What are you stressed about?" she asked.

"This." Lily held up the flyer. "Can you put it up somewhere?"

"Yes." Seren's eyes lit up as she took the paper. "Yay! You have a date. Why are you stressed? You should be excited."

"Tell that to my nervous system. Apparently, all I can focus on are the things that could go wrong."

"Nothing will go wrong," Seren said. "Are you going to employ someone to help out?"

"I don't know." She had pondered the idea, but then she'd put it out of her head and forgot to come back to it. "Maybe." Her eyes flashed to Flynn. "Should I?"

"Sorry," Seren said. "I didn't mean to cause you more stress."

Lily pressed her lips together. "I don't know how busy it will be so it's hard to judge if I'll need someone or not."

"You can wait and see how the first couple of weeks go," Flynn said. "Then employ someone if you need help. I'll help on opening day."

"Me too," Seren said.

"Thanks." She exhaled a dramatic breath. "I think I need a drink."

They ordered food as well, deciding they'd earned a pub lunch, then chatted with Seren in between her serving customers.

"I wanted to ask you something," Lily said across the bar once they'd finished eating.

"What is it?" Seren asked.

"What do you know about Glynis?" Lily scrunched her nose up, realising she didn't know her last name or much about her at all. "You know the woman who calls into the shop for ice creams in the mornings?"

"Glynis Ward? She's such a sweetie. And she's totally my role model. I want to be her when I'm in my eighties. I swear she's fitter than I am."

"She's great," Lily said. "Do you happen to have her

phone number? I haven't seen her in a few days, and she specifically said she'd be coming into the shop. I'm a little worried about her."

Seren shook her head. "I don't have her number, but I could probably find it out. I know where she lives."

"That works," Lily said. "I can call in and check she's okay."

"I hope she's all right." Seren got her phone out to send Lily the address. "Now that you mention it, I haven't seen her in a few days either, which is unusual."

"I'm sure she's fine," Lily said. "And she has a carer living with her, so it's not as though she's alone."

"A carer?" Seren's eyebrows inched upwards. "Are we talking about the same person? I reckon Glynis would have strong objections to needing a carer."

"She introduced me to her at the garden centre the other day." Lily frowned as she tried to recall her name. "Maria. I think she said she's just been helping Glynis for a few months."

"Okay, that's even more worrying. Maybe her health isn't as good as she claims."

"I'll call in and check on her," Lily said as the message came through with the address.

Chapter Seven

IN THE END, Lily waited until the following day before she went in search of Glynis. She didn't have to go far. The quaint cottage on the outskirts of Hugh Town was only a five-minute walk from the ice cream shop. With her mind on the upcoming opening of the shop, she was almost at the house when she registered the ambulance parked outside.

A jolt of concern twisted her stomach, and she quickened her pace. Her eyes snagged on the dark-haired woman standing in the open doorway.

"Hi," Lily called out as she reached the front path. "We met the other day at the garden centre. Maria, isn't it?"

"Yes." Maria glanced over her shoulder, into the house, then her eyes darted back to Lily. "Can I help you with something?"

"I'm looking for Glynis. She hasn't been to visit me for a few days and I wanted to check on her." Her eyes darted to the ambulance. "Is she okay?"

"She's ill." Maria shifted her weight, her hands fidgeting on the strap of the large bag slung over her shoulder. "Now's not a good time."

"What happened?" Lily asked, looking around Maria into the house.

Reaching into her blouse, Maria pulled out a delicate gold chain and clutched at the pendant. "She's been ill for a few days. Some kind of stomach bug."

"Is it serious?"

Maria gave a twitchy shake of her head. "The doctor wants her to go into the hospital so she can monitor her."

"That doesn't sound great."

"She hasn't been able to keep anything down, so the doctor was concerned about dehydration." Her voice wobbled. "I'm sure she'll be fine."

"Are you okay?" Lily asked. "You look exhausted."

"I haven't slept much the last couple of nights." Her fingers worried at the pendant – a gold crucifix. "At least if she's in hospital, I'll know she's well cared for and I'll be able to catch up on some rest."

"Yes," Lily said, distracted by the paramedics bringing Glynis out on a stretcher.

"Not that I want her to be in hospital," Maria said in a rush.

"Of course not." Lily stepped off the path to give the para-medics room. Her jaw tightened as her eyes landed on Glynis. With her pale skin and dark rings under her eyes, she looked as though she'd aged about twenty years since Lily had last seen her.

"Lily," she murmured, her wrinkled arm creeping out from under the blanket.

Automatically, Lily took her hand and walked beside the stretcher. "I got worried when you didn't visit. I came to check on you."

"That's sweet," she said, through cracked lips. "I'm sure I'll be up to tasting your ice cream again soon."

Lily nodded. "They'll take good care of you at the hospital. You'll be up and about again in no time."

"Save me some ice cream," she murmured as her eyes fluttered closed.

"I will." Lily squeezed her hand and stepped away so the paramedics could get her into the ambulance. "Is there anything I can do?" she asked Maria, who was locking the door.

She shook her head and hurried past Lily. "I don't think so."

Lily wanted to ask her to keep her updated, but Maria had hopped up into the ambulance with Glynis and the doors had closed before she could get a word out.

Watching the ambulance go, Lily remained rooted to the spot. When she eventually snapped out of her trance and got her legs moving, she pulled out her phone to call Flynn.

"Glynis is ill," she said, bypassing greetings.

"What's wrong with her?"

"Apparently a stomach bug, but it must be pretty bad since she's just been taken to the hospital in an ambulance."

"Poor Glynis."

"Yeah. Where are you?"

"At home. Getting ready for work."

Lily stepped off the pavement to avoid a woman and her dog. "It's weird that we were both ill," she mused quietly.

"What?" Flynn asked.

"I was ill too, remember? Not as bad as Glynis, but also a stomach thing."

"Maybe there's something going round."

"We shared a drink at the garden centre." She grimaced, hoping Flynn would tell her she was being neurotic, and that she wasn't to blame for Glynis being in hospital. "Maybe I passed on my germs."

"Possibly," he said, making Lily's stomach lurch. "It's hardly your fault, though. You didn't know you were going to get ill. And that could just be a coincidence."

Taking a deep breath, Lily felt a little better. "She looked terrible."

"I'm sure she'll be okay."

"I hope so. I don't even know how to check up on her."

"If I have time later, I can call at the hospital and see if I can get an update."

"That'd be good. Let me know if you do."

He promised he would and told her he'd talk to her later.

Over the course of the day, Lily frequently reminded herself that Flynn would let her know if he found anything out. She tried calling the hospital herself but couldn't get any information from the receptionist.

The sun was on its slow descent towards the horizon and Lily was curled in her armchair watching the waves roll onto Porthcressa Beach when she spotted Flynn wandering along the promenade in his uniform. In a flash, she was out of the chair and heading downstairs.

"Did you find anything out about Glynis?" she asked as she opened the door to the shop.

His grimace caused a deep sense of dread to unfurl in Lily's stomach. "She's in intensive care, so I couldn't see her, but she's not doing great."

"She's going to be okay, though?" She opened the door wider, but Flynn made no move to come inside.

"The doctor's concerned about her heart."

"What?" Lily frowned deeply. "I thought it was a stomach bug."

"It's not clear what it is, but it's causing an abnormal heart rhythm. Though, the doctor said that could also be because of dehydration. They're monitoring her for now and treating the symptoms. They're also running some tests to figure out exactly what it is. And they have a helicopter on standby to take her to the mainland if she doesn't improve in the next twenty-four hours. Or if things get worse."

"That's terrible." Pressing a hand to her chest, Lily inhaled deeply. "I thought it was the same as what I had, but this sounds far worse."

"Given her age, maybe whatever it is has just affected her more severely."

Lily's eyes bulged. "So you think I gave her this?"

"No." He offered a sympathetic smile. "I wasn't blaming you, but I asked when her symptoms started and it was the same night you were ill. Which seems like a weird coincidence. There's no way to know for definite though, and it doesn't really matter, anyway."

"Except now I feel horribly guilty."

"It's not your fault," he said, tilting his head. "And now that she's in the hospital Glynis will probably be back to full health in no time."

"I hope so." She tipped her head. "Are you coming in?"

"I need to get back to the station, but I'll talk to you later."

As he walked away, Lily wrapped her arms around her middle and stared across the promenade at the deserted beach.

No matter what Flynn said, she knew guilt would continue to gnaw at her.

She only hoped Glynis would make a speedy recovery.

Chapter Eight

Worrying over Glynis gave Lily a disrupted night of sleep. Without a lot of hope, she called the hospital as soon as she woke to see if she could get any information. This time the receptionist on duty was much more sympathetic. While she wouldn't go into details, she told Lily that Glynis's condition was stable. That was a relief, at least.

According to hospital policy, only immediate family could visit her in intensive care, but as Lily ended the call, she'd already decided to try her luck in person later. First, she needed to collect her order from the garden centre.

A delivery on her doorstep made her stop on her way out of the door.

Curiously, she picked up the cellophane-wrapped basket to read the tag. The typed writing welcomed her to the island, but gave no indication of who it was from. Peering through the wrapping at the assortment of foods, Lily suspected it was from the owner of the shop. It wouldn't be the first time she'd left something for Lily – there'd been a note when she'd first looked around the shop, and more recently a file containing ice cream recipes.

A pang of irritation gripped Lily as she returned inside to deposit the basket in the back room. If the owner wanted to be in touch, it would be much easier if she'd be upfront about it. The anonymous messages were getting tedious.

Putting it out of her mind, she set off across the island. Bright blue skies and gentle gusts made it a pleasant trip, which lifted her mood. She even felt a tingle of excitement about finally opening the shop.

It faded as soon as she reached the garden centre and was once again faced with the realisation that she didn't really know what she was doing.

"It's more than I thought," she told Gordon, who had everything ready and waiting for her.

"This is what we discussed on the phone," he said. "But—"

Lily cut him off. "It's great. I didn't mean it's too much. I just didn't think about how I'd carry it." It wouldn't be heavy, but the trays of raspberries and strawberries needed to be kept flat, which would make them awkward to carry across the island.

"Are you on foot?" Gordon asked.

"Yes. I don't have a car."

"I can give you a lift."

"Thanks," Lily said. "I'll need to figure something out in the future." Maybe she could get a bike with a trailer.

"We can also deliver, if you'd like."

"That would be great," Lily said. "I'd obviously pay a delivery fee."

Gordon waved a hand dismissively.

"Hi!" Sally said, striding outside and placing an affectionate hand between Lily's shoulder blades. "I saw a flyer about the opening of the ice cream shop. It's exciting."

Lily forced a smile. "Yeah."

"Do you have a spare poster?" Sally asked. "We could put one up here."

"Not on me. I have extras back at the shop."

"I'll grab one when I drop you off," Gordon said. "Us small businesses need to help each other out whenever we can."

"You've already been very helpful," Lily said. "I really appreciate it."

"Have you got time for a drink before you head off?" Sally asked.

Lily's eyes drifted inside and she thought of the green smoothie. Immediately, her stomach clenched in protest. It wasn't the smoothie that had made her ill, though. Was it? Could you get food poisoning from a smoothie? It seemed unlikely.

"I've got to get going," she said weakly. "I have a busy week of making ice cream ahead of me and I want to get started."

Sally bunched her shoulder up as she smiled. "Another time. I'll see you for the opening if not before. I can't wait to try the ice cream."

"Thanks," Lily mumbled as Sally waltzed away again.

Gordon had just lifted the tray of raspberries when Denzel walked over, a pair of gardening gloves hanging limply out of his back pocket.

"Need a hand?" He didn't wait for a reply before picking up the tray of strawberries and bag of lemons.

Gordon glanced over at him. "I'm just going to drive Lily home with this lot."

"I'm heading to Hugh Town," Denzel said, flashing Lily a smile. "I can drop you off."

"Thanks," Lily said, uncomfortable with the feeling of needing help. "If you don't mind."

"Not at all."

They loaded everything into Denzel's truck and Lily thanked Gordon before they set off.

"I can't believe the ice cream shop is finally going to open again," Denzel said as they pulled away along the narrow road.

"Do you remember it from before?" Lily asked, turning in her seat and watching his features.

"Yeah. That feels like a lifetime ago. It kind of was. Most of your lifetime, anyway."

"Yeah."

"I heard you'd been there as a kid," he said, keeping his eyes on the road.

"Yes." She frowned, wondering where he'd heard that, and how much more he knew about her.

It was one of the most unnerving things about living in such a close-knit community – people often knew things about her before they met her. Though, she supposed that was also partly her own fault for making such a name for herself by stumbling into investigating crimes.

"So you came back looking for the ice cream shop?" Denzel asked, the skin around his eyes crinkling.

"Yes. I had memories of it and wanted to see if it was still there." She turned further in her seat, pulling on the seatbelt when she met resistance. "Do you remember the woman who owned it?"

"Vaguely."

"I have a photo of her," Lily said, pulling it out of her bag.

Denzel nodded. "That's her."

"Have you seen her since the ice cream shop closed?"

"Not to my recollection. You think she lives on St Mary's, right?"

"How do you know that?"

He shrugged. "People talk."

Lily stared out of the window at the green fields.

"It'd be strange if she was around and watching you, but keeping quiet. Why would she do that?"

"I've no idea." Lily knew it sounded absurd, but her gut told her that the owner wasn't far away. That, and the fact that she'd left Lily a note in the shop, and then the recipes. And apparently a basket of food now, too.

"I hope it works out for you with the shop," Denzel said wistfully as the fields on either side of the road were replaced by rows of houses at the edge of Hugh Town. "It's the perfect spot for an ice cream shop. It'll be good to see some bustle down that end of the promenade after the place has been in such a rundown state for so long. Odd, though, isn't it?" His voice took on a faraway quality, as though he were thinking aloud.

"What is?"

Creases lined his brow. "That the owner wouldn't let a local re-open the shop. There was interest in the place before you came along."

"Yeah." Lily rolled her eyes. "Kit Treneary wanted to buy the place. He reminds me often enough."

"You know Kit?" Denzel paused and gave a small shake of the head. "Of course you know Kit." He looked as though he might say more, but remained silent as he parked behind a small van. "I think this is as close as I can get," he said, unbuckling his seatbelt. "I'll help you carry it to your door."

"Thank you," Lily said, hopping out to unload with him.

They were walking along the promenade with their hands

full when Lily spotted Kit wandering towards them, his sandy blonde hair being ruffled by the sea breeze.

"Hey!" he called out and picked up his pace to take a shopping bag that was swinging from Lily's finger. He frowned down at it. "I thought I was being heroic, but this weighs nothing at all."

"It's fresh mint for my mint choc ice cream," Lily told him. "Nothing is heavy, but some of it's awkward to carry. Thankfully, Denzel drove me from the garden centre."

He smiled a greeting at Denzel and they continued three abreast along the promenade.

"If you ever need a car," Kit said. "You're welcome to borrow ours."

"*Ours?*" Denzel said with an amused lilt.

Kit chuckled. "Obviously, no one should mention to Seren that I referred to it as *our* car. It's *hers*. But you're still welcome to borrow it."

"Thanks," Lily said. "Gordon said he can deliver in future, so I think I should be okay."

"How's work?" Kit asked Denzel when they stopped in front of the shop and Lily balanced the raspberries to retrieve her key.

"Same old," Denzel told him. "Keeps me out of mischief."

"If you have time, could you call over and give me some advice about our garden?" Kit asked.

"Yeah." Denzel shifted his weight. "Sorry, I told you I'd do that ages ago. It's my busiest time of year at the moment. Life's been hectic."

"No worries," Kit said. "You can also just call over for a coffee. I don't think you've seen the decking since we finished it. And you won't have seen the new bathroom upstairs."

Lily finally got the door open and held it for Denzel and Kit.

"I'll pop in sometime," Denzel said vaguely.

"Any time," Kit told him. "Just call over."

"I'll try." Denzel slid the tray of strawberries onto the counter. "I'm afraid I have to dash off. I was on my way to a job."

"Thanks for your help," Lily said, setting the raspberries down.

At the door, he raised a hand to wave and was gone without another word.

"I think I annoyed him," Kit said.

"Denzel?" Lily asked. "I take it you know him well?"

"Yeah. I've known him for as long as I can remember. He used to work with my dad sometimes."

"Why would he be annoyed with you?"

"When Seren I and first got the house, he used to come and help me out with renovations. We needed all the help we could get, so I always took him up on any offer to help, but I may have asked too often because recently he always makes excuses." His shoulders rose and fell as he sighed. "I don't even care about him helping. I just enjoyed hanging out with him. He has all these stories about my dad that I've never heard before." He shrugged. "I liked hearing his stories."

"I imagine that would be nice." For a moment, Lily's thoughts drifted to her own parents. "I barely remember my parents, and I don't know anyone who knew them. It'd be nice to hear stories about them."

"Sorry," Kit said. "I didn't mean to bring the mood down."

"It's fine." She smiled sadly. "I get it, though. I'll bet it's interesting to hear about your dad from someone who isn't family. Denzel would have known a different side to your dad, I guess."

"Yeah." Kit nodded emphatically. "That's exactly it."

"He said he was busy," Lily remarked. "I'm sure it's just that."

"Maybe." Kit didn't sound convinced. "Anyway, I was on my way to meet Seren for lunch. Do you want to join us?"

"I'd better not." She gestured to the fruit on the counter-top. "I have a lot of work to do."

She'd make a couple of batches of ice cream, then she'd head over to the hospital and see if she could get an update on Glynis.

Chapter Nine

"COULD I just see her for a few minutes?" Lily pleaded with the grey-haired receptionist at the hospital who'd refused to give her any information.

"I'm sorry, but I can only let immediate family in."

"Does Glynis even have immediate family on the island?" Lily asked, leaning onto the desk.

"Unfortunately not." The soft voice drew Lily's attention to the doctor in a white coat, who smiled as she approached. "Her son has been in touch, but he lives in Manchester and can't make it over here in the next few days."

Lily straightened. "Surely having visitors would be good for her."

"I agree." The woman extended her hand. "Dr. Laura Redwood."

"I'm Lily." She shook her hand. "Can I see Glynis then?"

She nodded and led the way along the corridor. "You shouldn't stay long," she said as she went. "But I think a visit might lift her spirits."

"How's she doing?"

"She's stable now, so I'm hoping that with some more rest,

we'll see improvements soon." She opened the door and gestured for Lily to go in. "Five minutes. Okay?"

"Thank you," Lily said as the doctor turned to leave. Slowly, she approached the bed.

Glynis's eyelids fluttered open. "I was expecting Maria," she said, her voice hoarse. "What time is it?"

Lily checked her watch. "Almost three."

"I don't know why Maria hasn't been to see me."

"Wasn't she here this morning?"

"No. She said she'd come, but she didn't."

"She'll no doubt be here soon. The receptionist is a bit of a stickler for the rules, though. She didn't want to let me in because I'm not family."

"They said they'd make an exception for Maria." Her words were slow and her breathing laboured. "It's nice to see you, anyway."

"How are you feeling?" Lily asked, forcing herself not to react to how frail she looked.

"A little better than yesterday, I think."

"That's good. The doctor seems nice. I'm sure she'll have you back to your old self in no time."

"Hope so," Glynis murmured as her eyes closed.

"I should go and let you rest," Lily said. "Is there anything you need?"

She turned her head from side to side on the pillow and Lily gave her hand a quick squeeze.

"Oh, there's one thing," Glynis croaked, opening her eyes again. "Could you check on Maria? I'm worried about her."

"Of course. Do you have your phone? I can call and see when she's planning to visit?"

Glynis's gaze roamed over the room. "I don't know."

After a quick search, Lily located it in a bag in the

wardrobe. With Glynis's help, she found Maria's number and hit dial.

"There's no answer," she said after letting it ring.

"Very strange." Glynis's eyes were filled with concern. "I don't suppose..."

Lily smiled. "I'll go to the house and check on her." She also saved the phone numbers for both Maria and Glynis to her phone. "I'm sure she's fine."

"Thank you." Glynis reached out a trembling hand.

"You're welcome," Lily said, giving her hand another squeeze, then tucking it back under the covers. "I'll call you when I've spoken to her, or get her to call." She set the phone on the table where Glynis could reach it. Then she instructed her to rest and closed the door quietly behind her when she left.

It was odd that Maria hadn't been in touch. At the reception desk Lily wanted to ask if she'd at least been in touch for an update, but the receptionist was on the phone, and a peaky-looking woman was waiting to speak to her.

Outside, Lily tried to call Maria again, hoping she could save herself a trip over there, but again, there was no answer.

Fifteen minutes later, a tingle of trepidation stirred in her stomach as she stood on the doorstep of Glynis's house and raised her hand to knock for the second time. Impatiently, she stepped into the neat front garden and cupped her hands against the windowpane to peer into the living room.

Noise from inside had her hurrying back to the path.

Slowly, the door eased open to reveal Maria in a pair of floral pyjamas.

"Are you okay?" Lily blurted out, shocked by her sickly pallor.

"I don't know." She made an attempt at smoothing down

her wayward tufts of hair. When her eyes came back to Lily, they flashed with panic. "I'm so sorry."

"Sorry for what?" Lily frowned in concern.

"Someone's out to get us," she muttered, eyes darting along the road. "This can't be happening. And I got Glynis caught up in all this too. I don't even know if she's okay." Again, her gaze came back to Lily. "I tried calling the hospital, but no one answered... I wasn't up to going out."

"Glynis is okay," Lily said. "Are you ill too?"

Maria nodded and clutched at the pendant at the base of her throat.

"It must be some sort of virus," Lily said. "One which is highly contagious."

"No." Maria's brow wrinkled and her eyes flickered with fear. "That's not what it is. Someone is out to get us."

Lily cocked her head. "Should I call the doctor? You seem a little confused."

"They're not going to stop until we're dead," she muttered, the words barely audible. Her wild eyes snapped back to Lily, and she grabbed at her hand. "Come in quick, in case someone is watching."

She dragged Lily over the threshold before she could protest.

Chapter Ten

PUZZLED WAS AN UNDERSTATEMENT. Standing in the kitchen of the quaint, homely cottage, Lily was completely flummoxed. Maria's ramblings hadn't made an ounce of sense. She probably had a fever. It was the only way Lily could explain the paranoid mutterings which had been cut short by Maria dashing to the bathroom.

The sound of her retching drifted to the kitchen and Lily distracted herself by messaging Flynn to give him an update on Glynis.

Her phone rang almost as soon as she'd hit send.

"There's something really weird going on," Flynn said, an air of confusion to his words.

"How do you mean?" Lily asked, standing beside the kitchen table and gazing at a decorative bowl which held a few bananas and apples. Papers and envelopes lay scattered haphazardly beside the bowl.

"Have you seen the food baskets people have been posting about on social media? Wait, did you get one?"

Idly, Lily pushed her hip against the edge of the table. "I don't know what you're talking about."

"A bunch of residents received baskets of food on their doorsteps."

"Oh." Her spine straightened. "Yeah, I got one. I thought it was from the owner of the shop since it didn't say who it was from."

"You didn't eat anything from it, did you?"

"No. I barely even looked at it. Why?"

"Because it seems as though anyone who's eaten anything from it has got ill."

Lily sucked in a quick breath and swung around until her gaze landed on the wicker basket on the sideboard. Drifting over to it, she turned over the tag attached to the handle. "Welcome to the island," she muttered, reading the printed text aloud. The exact same message as her basket.

"Sorry?"

"Maria got one," she said. "Glynis's friend... carer... whatever she is. I'm at their place now and there's a basket. By the way, Glynis is stable. I saw her earlier."

"Good. But the basket... make sure you tell Maria not to eat anything from it."

Lily lifted the bag of pasta, which was half empty, and then eyed the open pouch of mixed herbs.

"I think it's too late for that," she said. "She's currently vomiting, and she looks deathly pale. What's going on?"

"As far as we know, they were delivered to about a dozen people across the island. They all have a welcome message, but don't indicate who they're from."

"So if they all have welcome messages, that means..."

"They were only delivered to newcomers to the island."

"All delivered anonymously?"

"Yeah."

"That's weird." She squinted at the message on the tag.

"At least that explains why Maria thinks someone is out to get us."

"What?"

"She was ranting, and I thought she meant that someone was out to get me and her specifically, but I guess she meant newcomers in general. She must have read about it on social media."

"What's in the basket Maria received?"

Her eyes roamed over the contents. "Fresh pasta, a bag of Italian herbs, loose leaf tea... a bar of chocolate..." Glancing around the room, she spotted a glass jar by the sink. "Possibly a jar of pasta sauce. I guess that's what she ate – the pasta and sauce."

"Sounds the same as all the others. Can you tell her not to touch it? I'll be over to collect it later. I'll need to call over and collect yours as well."

"Okay." Her mind whirred, trying to make sense of everything. "Do you think someone did this on purpose?"

"We don't know. The sergeant is assuming it's accidental poisoning, but it's weird that the baskets were delivered anonymously."

"And just to newcomers," Lily mused, a niggling feeling at the back of her mind. "Did you get one?"

"No. I don't know whether to be affronted at being left out, or happy that I wasn't subject to food poisoning."

"I'd choose the latter," she said, frowning at the basket on the counter. "Do you think maybe Dante was right?"

Flynn gave a quizzical grunt.

"The owner of the Italian restaurant." She paced the kitchen. "He thought someone wanted to sabotage him because he's not from the island."

"It's possible," Flynn said, but didn't sound convinced.

"I need to speak to him again."

"I'm working," Flynn said. "I've got to collect these baskets and question the recipients. I'm fairly sure the sergeant won't agree to me questioning Dante, at least not until I've finished with all of this."

"I wasn't inviting you," she teased. "But I will let you know what I find out."

"I'll talk to you later."

She'd just slipped her phone back into her pocket when Maria shuffled into the kitchen. "Sorry about that," she murmured, moving past Lily to get a glass of water.

"Do you need anything?"

She shook her head.

"I only just heard about the baskets," Lily told her. "I got one too, but I didn't eat anything from it, thank goodness."

"The smoothie was meant for you, wasn't it?"

Lily gave her a puzzled smile.

"I'm not blaming you," she whispered. "Of course it's not your fault, but Glynis got sick after she drank it. I thought about it when the doctor suggested Glynis might have food poisoning rather than a virus. That's the only thing she consumed that I didn't. We eat all our meals together. You gave the smoothie to her, didn't you? It was meant for you, not Glynis."

"Yes, but..." Lily stared at her, confused. "I don't understand. You think the person who delivered the welcome baskets also tried to poison me with the smoothie?"

She nodded meekly. "Maybe."

"You really think someone is out to get newcomers to the island?" Her mind went to the review Dante had shown her, commenting on foreigners taking jobs.

Maria only gazed at Lily, saying nothing.

"By the way, PC Grainger said he'll collect the basket

later. It sounds as though he has a few to collect, so it might take a while."

She tilted her head and creases marked her forehead. "How many people received them?"

"I'm not sure. I think he said a dozen." She retrieved her phone again. "He said it's all over social media. It's the sort of thing people like to post about on the community groups."

It didn't take Lily long to find people posting pictures of the welcome baskets. The posts from the previous evening were filled with gratitude and excitement, then turned ominous that morning, as people reported getting ill.

With her focus on her phone, Lily only noticed that Maria had moved across the room when she glanced up to find her shuffling the papers on the kitchen table with trembling hands.

"You should go and lie down," Lily said.

Frantically, she continued collecting up the papers. "It's such a mess. With Glynis being ill, and now me, I haven't had much time for cleaning."

"Leave it for now," Lily said, watching her shove the papers into a drawer in the mahogany dresser. "You can worry about that when you're better."

Finally, Maria looked up at Lily. "Lots of people got ill?" she asked.

"Yes. Quite a few. Anyone who ate anything from the baskets."

Maria pressed her fingers to her forehead. "I don't know what I was thinking, eating something without knowing where it had come from. But I'd been at the hospital with Glynis and it was late when I got home. I hadn't eaten..."

"I'd have done the same," Lily said, aiming for a reassuring tone.

"Why would someone target newcomers to the island?" Maria asked, slumping into a chair.

"I don't know. I think I'll dig around, see what I can find out..."

"Yes. Good idea." Again, she reached into the neckline of her pyjamas and squeezed on her crucifix.

"Are you religious?"

She looked at Lily with complete bewilderment. "No. Why?"

"Never mind," Lily said, shaking her head. "Do you think you'll be okay alone?"

"I'll be fine." She looked distracted. "You should go."

"I'll call you later and see how you're doing."

"Yes," she said vaguely. "Okay."

Chapter Eleven

It DIDN'T TAKE LONG for Dante to open the door to the restaurant. When he did, it was with his phone held aloft.

"Have you seen this?" he asked Lily as he waved it around. "Didn't I tell you someone is sabotaging me? I came to see you earlier, but you weren't at your shop."

"I've been out most of the day," she told him, homing in on the phone screen, only to find it had gone to the screensaver.

"Good. You're working on the case then? Do you know who's poisoning people?"

"No. What's on the phone?"

"It's all over social media," he said. "People wrote posts about the lovely welcome baskets they got." He clicked on a post and brought up a photo. "And then someone posted that they got ill after they drank tea from their basket. Now more people are ill. It's just like here in the restaurant."

"It definitely doesn't feel like a coincidence."

"What have you found out so far?" he demanded.

"Not much." She didn't like to admit that she'd only just begun to take his complaint seriously. "What I would like to know is who wrote the bad review for the restaurant. The one that mentioned foreigners taking the jobs on the island."

"I'd like to know too," Dante said determinedly. "That's why I hired you."

"You didn't actually hire me," Lily murmured. "Never mind. I think there must be a link between the reviewer and the person who sent the baskets. It seems logical, anyway, since the baskets were only sent to newcomers on the island."

"How can we find out who it is?" Dante stared at her as though she had all the answers.

"Is it possible you remember who was in the restaurant the evening you got the review? Or around that time. Do you have a reservation list?"

"Yes." He beckoned her into the kitchen and opened a hefty book on the table. "This is the reservation book, but if someone just came on the evening I won't have a record of it." He paused, looking thoughtful. "I already thought about it, but they were all very nice people, so I thought it might have been someone else who'd been in on a different day. Maybe they didn't write the review straight away."

"That's a possibility." Lily leaned to look at the relevant page in the reservation book, but struggled to read the handwriting.

"This is a teacher at the school," Dante said, jabbing the book. "Came with her husband. Very nice couple. Can't be anything to do with them."

"You can't rule people out just because they're nice."

"Fine," he said. "Maybe it's them, but I don't believe it." He pressed his finger onto the next name. "Zac Wheeler. He's a fisherman. Supplies me lovely fresh fish. Great guy."

"He definitely has the means of sabotaging you, doesn't he?"

"With his fish? No way. They're fresh and beautiful, and I already told you he's a great guy."

"It would be helpful if you could keep an open mind."

He shook his head and trailed his finger down a line. "Mr Pengelly. Also, a great guy. Brought his staff in for dinner."

"Wait, that's Gordon from the garden centre?"

"Yes. Now don't start accusing him. He's been helping me get set up. No way he'd try to harm my business."

"But I got ill after I drank a smoothie from the garden centre," Lily said animatedly. "Who was he with when he came for dinner?"

"I told you – his staff."

"Who is that?"

"Gordon and his daughter. She's very sweet."

Lily nodded. "I've met Sally."

"Then there's the rough-looking guy. A workman or gardener, a bit younger than me. Maybe fifty or so."

"Denzel?"

"Yes. Denzel! And a tall man who smiles a lot. Very jolly. Like an overgrown little boy."

"Arthur," Lily surmised.

"Yes. He's a funny guy." Dante scratched his head. "Now don't tell me you think one of them poisoned my customers."

She inhaled through her nose, trying not to lose her patience. "Could any of them have come into the kitchen at all?"

"I gave them a tour," Dante said with a nod. "Not that they'd need to sneak into the kitchen if they want to sabotage me."

"How do you mean?"

"Gordon supplies me with a lot of fresh food. Vegetables and fruits and some herbs."

Lily huffed out a humourless laugh. "That's definitely

dodgy. Glynis and I got ill from the smoothie at the garden centre and your customers are ill after eating food supplied by them. Either someone there is up to something, or someone is tampering with their goods."

"No one there would do such a thing," Dante insisted.

Lily patted his arm. "Not all villains look like villains."

"I just don't believe you," he said.

"Let me look into it further," she said. "There's definitely something fishy going on."

Dante threw his hands up. "Now you want to blame the fisherman?"

"No." Lily smothered a smile. "It's just a saying. I'll get back to you, okay?"

"Yes. I rely on you, Lily."

She drew in a deep breath as she strode out of the restaurant. Ambling along Church Street, she mulled everything over.

She tended not to believe in coincidences. Which meant she was keen to do a bit of sniffing around. If she could find a connection to the welcome baskets, she could pin all these incidents of poisoning on the garden centre.

With her investigative juices flowing, she told herself not to be so suspicious. Even if everything was linked, it didn't mean there was anything sinister at play. Most likely, it was an honest mistake.

The fact that the baskets had been delivered anonymously didn't necessarily mean anything. Maybe the benefactor merely wanted to do a good deed without any attention.

But there was also the restaurant review complaining about newcomers...

She wondered if she was right to be suspicious or if her recent investigations had left her with a tendency to assume the worst.

With a desire to pay another visit to the garden centre, she checked the opening times on her phone, then frowned when she calculated that she wouldn't make it across the island in time.

Flynn added a fifth basket to the back of the Land Rover. He'd just closed the door when he caught sight of Lily across the road. He almost called out to her, but stopped himself at the last second.

She'd been walking slowly, but came to a sudden stop as though her batteries had worn out. After a quick shake of her head, she started up again, but only made it a few steps before standing still again. The shifts in her facial expressions gave the impression she was engaged in some deep mental conversation.

In the bright sunshine her chestnut hair looked lighter than usual, and when she hooked it behind her ear, the tightness of her jaw was visible even from the other side of the road. The tension in her features contrasted with her casual attire of low hung jeans and tight T-shirt with a logo so faded it was no longer recognisable.

He should really call out and make his presence known, but her lack of awareness was strangely captivating.

She set off again, then paused and pulled her phone from her pocket. Her eyebrows pulled together as she glared at whatever had offended her on the screen.

Finally, Flynn forced himself into action and jogged across the narrow street, pressing the fob to lock the Land Rover as he went.

Even when he sidled up beside her, she didn't register him.

"Do you ever think about looking where you're going?"

At his words, her face whipped up to meet his gaze, then she glanced all around as though reacquainting herself with her surroundings.

"Where did you come from?" she asked.

"I just collected a basket. You were miles away."

She stared up at him. "You didn't get a basket," she stated firmly.

"Nope."

"Why not?" she demanded.

He lifted an eyebrow. "Is that rhetorical, or are you expecting me to know why I was left out?"

"I'd like to know." She pressed her lips together, seeming deep in thought again. "If someone was delivering baskets to newcomers to the island, why would they skip you?"

"Maybe I've offended them?" he suggested.

"That's a fair possibility," she agreed, a little too fervently for his liking. "But what if it's not *you* they have an issue with, but your profession."

"You think someone didn't give me a basket because they don't like the police?"

She shook her head. "I think they drew the line at poisoning a police officer. If you were committing a crime, maybe you wouldn't want to commit a crime against a police officer, right?"

"Wait..." He pursed his lips. "What did I miss? Why are you assuming the poisonings were intentional?"

"Several reasons, but I'm not sure of anything yet. I need to look into it further."

"I need to get the basket from you and then head back to the station."

He decided it was as easy to walk to the shop with her

than take the car. On the way, she told him about her visit to Dante and the restaurant's connection to the garden centre.

"You could be on to something," he agreed when they arrived at the shop and she finally stopped talking.

"Or I could be making connections which aren't really there..."

"They're definitely there. It's worth looking into." They stepped inside and went to the back of the shop. "I could mention it to the sergeant and see what he thinks."

She shook her head. "I wouldn't mention the garden centre just yet. Tell him about the restaurant review if you want."

"What are you going to do?" he asked as he retrieved the basket from the counter in the back room.

"I'm going to pay a visit to the garden centre tomorrow and see if I can find a link between that place and the welcome baskets."

Of course she was.

Smiling, he wished her luck and made her promise to keep him updated.

Thanks to her information, his afternoon collecting food baskets felt a lot more worthwhile now. As much as she doubted herself, he was sure she was onto something. With any luck the sergeant would agree.

Chapter Twelve

CONSIDERING IT WAS SATURDAY, the garden centre was surprisingly quiet when Lily arrived in the middle of the morning. An elderly couple arrived at the same time as her and smiled before setting off to wander the outside area. Lily went in the other direction, walking slowly and hoping something might jump out at her as being out of place.

She was contemplating how she might go about subtly questioning the staff as she made her way inside.

The till inside the entrance was unmanned and her eyes lingered on the assortment of ribbons in a dispenser at the edge of the desk. The welcome baskets had been tied with ribbon. She smiled to herself, thinking how convenient it would be to catch someone with an incriminating strip of ribbon. As though the person who'd put the baskets together might still have a piece trailing from their sleeve.

At the back of the building, the cafe was empty, though there were signs of life, with a laptop open on one table and a bunch of papers and notebooks spread around it. Instinct had Lily drifting in that direction, while glancing around, expecting the owner of the belongings to reappear at any moment.

"Hello!" she called, stopping beside the table. No reply came and her gaze dropped to the open notebook which overflowed with sketches of plants and flowers. She reached for a piece of paper as the words at the top jumped out at her.

"Poisonous plants in your garden," she muttered, reading aloud. "Lily of the valley, hydrangea, bluebell, foxglove, oleander, daffodil, ivy..." Her gaze snapped up before she'd finished the list. A chill rippled up her spine as she set the list down again.

Was this connected with the welcome baskets? And the smoothie?

"Hello?" Lily called again, venturing towards the counter at the back of the cafe.

"I'll be with you in a minute!"

The voice came from the direction of the office and sounded distinctly like Sally Pengelly.

Lily didn't wait for her, but drifted back there and gave a gentle knock on the door, which was slightly ajar.

"Sorry." Sally looked up from the computer screen. "It's been so quiet this morning that I slipped in here to get caught up on a few emails."

"It's fine," Lily said. "I just thought it was odd that there were no staff around."

"You haven't bumped into Denzel? He should be here somewhere."

"I haven't seen him."

"What are you after?" Sally asked, her warm persona practically oozing from her pores.

"How do you mean?"

Lily was hoping to nose around and see what she came up with, but she supposed that might not be so easy if people saw her as an investigator. That was probably why most investigators kept their identity anonymous. But that wasn't so easy when you lived on an island with less than two thousand residents.

"Houseplants, I assume?" Sally said as she rose from the chair.

"Yes," Lily replied, happy that Sally had assumed she was there to buy plants, rather than investigate. "I don't know anything about plants, though."

"I can help you pick some out. People tend to just go for what they like the look of, but that's usually a mistake." She passed Lily and walked into the cafe. As she talked animatedly about the different levels of care and attention plants needed, Lily trailed behind her, then stopped at the edge of the tables.

As though she'd imagined them entirely, the laptop and papers were gone.

"Everything okay?" Sally asked, turning back to Lily.

"Do you know who was in the cafe before?"

"We had a few customers first thing," Sally said, forehead crinkling. "No one I knew. Why?"

"There was a laptop on that table." She pointed. "And some papers. I was only in the office for a moment. How have they just vanished?" Her eyes scanned all around but there was no one to be seen. "You said Denzel was here? Would he have been working at one of the tables?"

"On a laptop?" Sally's lips twitched at the corners. "That would be very high tech for him. I mean, he has his own business, so you'd think he must have a laptop, but I wouldn't be surprised if he didn't. The man doesn't even have a smart phone. If you want to speak to him, you have to call him. It's quite annoying that he won't message or email."

"Who would have been sitting here with a laptop?" Lily

asked, annoyed at herself for giving the person time to pack up and leave without her clocking them.

"I couldn't tell you." Sally looked a little unnerved by Lily's frantic tone. "Arthur was here earlier, but I think he left a while ago."

"*Someone* was here," Lily said, setting off towards the exit. "They were just here!"

Outside, she dodged around plants, her eyes darting manically as she searched for the person who'd been researching poisonous plants. They couldn't have gone far, but when she reached the car park, there was no sign of anyone.

"Lily!" Sally called, following at a gentle run. She stopped right in front of Lily and grabbed at her upper arms. "Are you okay?" she asked breathlessly.

"Yeah." Lily continued to glance around, sure that there must be someone lurking nearby.

"Do you feel all right?" Sally asked, staring directly into Lily's eyes.

"I feel fine," Lily replied, backing away and shrugging Sally off. "What are you doing?"

"I don't want to panic you, but can you tell me if you received a basket of goodies to welcome you to the island?"

Lily raised an eyebrow. "Why?"

"Because some people got ill from the stuff in the baskets. Most of the symptoms were stomach related, but I think I heard someone mention confusion." She looked at Lily sympathetically. "You're acting a little odd."

"Oh." Lily stifled a laugh. "It's nothing like that. I got a basket, but didn't eat anything from it. Maybe I'm just on high alert because of it. And the papers on the table..." She trailed off, not sure how much she wanted to share with Sally. "It was odd how they were there and then gone."

"You're sure you're feeling okay?" Sally asked.

"Yes." Lily dragged in a deep breath. "Does anyone else work here? Is there a cook for the cafe or anything?"

Sally gave a small shake of her head. "The sandwiches and cakes are delivered each morning. Whoever is here first makes a batch of smoothies. Usually two different ones, but it's not a lot of work. We keep things simple."

"So it's just the four of you working here? You, your dad, Arthur and Denzel?"

"Yes." Her lips pulled to a bemused smile. "What's with all the questions?"

"Sorry," Lily said. "I guess all this talk of poisoning on social media has got me a little rattled. I think I'll come back and look for plants another day." She definitely couldn't concentrate on anything now, and it would be good to have an excuse to come back.

"Take care," Sally said as Lily walked away. Her voice carried its usual sweetness, but somehow the words sounded ominous to Lily's ears.

She quickened her steps to get away from the place.

Chapter Thirteen

THE MESSAGE from Seren came through just as Lily put her key in the lock back at the shop. She muttered a curse, remembering that she'd promised to let her know if she found out anything about Glynis. From the doorstep she fired off a quick message saying Glynis was stable and that she'd seen her, then asked where Seren was. Hopefully, she might have time for a chat, since Lily could do with a sounding board.

When a reply came immediately to say she was working at the pub, Lily removed her key from the lock and turned on her heel.

She arrived at the Mermaid Inn a few minutes later.

"Sorry," she said to Seren while sliding onto a bar stool. "I meant to message you yesterday, but my day got crazy."

"No worries." Seren continued to pour drinks. "How was Glynis when you saw her?"

"She didn't look good, but the doctor didn't seem overly concerned."

"Mirren just left to visit her." Seren paused and tipped her head to one side. "She was sure you must be wrong about

Glynis having a carer. She didn't know anything about it, and she chats to Glynis regularly."

Lily smiled, imagining how put out Mirren Treneary would be about not being on top of island news. "She definitely has someone living with her. Apparently Maria is an old friend."

"How long did you say she's she been living with Glynis?"

Lily shrugged. "I think she said a few months."

"Weird. Glynis didn't mention anything to me, but maybe she doesn't want to ruin her reputation. Being so independent is a part of her identity."

"Makes sense," Lily said. "Apparently Maria is also shy. Glynis told me she was worried about her not socialising." She watched as Seren expertly topped up a pint of Guinness. "I guess she'll be hiding away at home for longer now, since she's also ill."

Seren grimaced. "Same thing as Glynis?"

"I don't know." Lily frowned. "Did you hear about the welcome baskets that made people ill?"

"Yes! Everyone's been talking about it today. Crazy, isn't it?" Her eyes widened. "Did you get one?"

"Yes, but thankfully I didn't touch anything in it."

Seren shook her head, causing a lock of red hair to fall from her messy bun. "Can you image trying to do a good deed and then making people ill? Whoever sent them must feel terrible. I wonder if they'll come forward."

"I don't think it was an accident," Lily whispered.

Seren narrowed her eyes as she loaded the drinks onto a tray. "How do you mean?"

"I think someone deliberately delivered contaminated food. They wanted to make people ill."

"Why would someone do that?" Seren's eyes shone with disbelief.

"I'm not entirely sure, but I think someone has a grudge against newcomers to the island."

"Are you serious?"

Lily gave a curt nod and took out her phone, clicking into the reviews of Dante's restaurant. "I think the person who delivered the baskets also tried to sabotage Dante's business."

She wrinkled her nose. "*Who?*"

"Dante Accardi. He owns the new Italian restaurant. His food has been making people ill, and he asked me to look into it. I didn't think much of it at first." She handed the phone to Seren, showing the review which bothered her the most. "I'd really like to find out who posted this."

Seren chewed on her lip as she scanned the review. "The Secret B," she muttered, reading the name of the reviewer.

"I don't suppose you have any idea who it could be?"

"I do, actually." Seren handed the phone back. "Do an internet search for The Secret Botanist. Add Isles of Scilly into the search and see what pops up. I'll be right back." She slid the tray from the bar and set off across the room.

Lily typed frantically on her phone, then clicked on the first link that came up. The blog was a simple layout with a banner across the top of the page and a list of hyperlinked blog post titles, each with a thumbnail picture of different plants. She clicked one entitled 'Edible Flowers' and immediately straightened her shoulders.

"What the heck is this?" she asked when Seren returned.

"The Secret Botanist is a local who blogs about gardening."

Lily's eyes bulged. "Whoever wrote this article was at the garden centre earlier. I saw a bunch of notes and sketches at the garden centre. The drawings were just like these." Lily angled the phone screen towards Seren.

"That makes sense."

"Does it?"

"Of course." She leaned against the bar. "The identity of the secret botanist is the island's worst kept secret. It's Arthur Penrose."

"Arthur from the garden centre?"

Seren nodded. "The blog has been going for years. At first he had some notions about keeping his identity a mystery. I'm not sure why. Anyway, since he can't stop talking about it, he didn't keep it a secret for long. He's very proud of it."

"He has a list of poisonous plants." A rush of adrenaline tingled through Lily. "Why would he have a list of poisonous plants?"

"For his blog, I imagine."

Lily clicked out of the blog post and scrolled through the list. She didn't scroll very far.

"Poisonous plants in your garden," she said, reading the heading aloud before she clicked into it. "Oh, my goodness." Her eyes skimmed over the text and accompanying sketches and photos. Alongside the common plants and flowers were the ways they could make you ill, including symptoms. "Someone is really poisoning people," Lily muttered.

"Lily!" Seren said, snapping her from her trance. "What are you talking about? Why do you think someone is poisoning people?"

"Because of Dante's restaurant, and then the welcome baskets being delivered anonymously."

"I think you need to slow down." Seren lowered her eyebrows. "Are you sure you're not getting carried away and seeing things that aren't there? Because this all seems pretty coincidental to me."

"I thought so at first as well," Lily said in a rush. "But I got ill too."

"You said you didn't eat anything in the basket."

"It was from a smoothie at the garden centre."

Seren pursed her lips. "How could you possibly know it was the smoothie that made you ill?"

"Because I shared it with Glynis. I think that's what made her ill."

"That's weird."

"Isn't it? I thought we just had a stomach bug until all these other people started getting ill."

Seren's eyes sparkled. "Actually, I meant it's weird that you share drinks with a little old lady. Couldn't you afford one each?"

"I had two sips and hated it," Lily explained with a smile. "So I gave it to Glynis to finish."

"Okay, that makes it less weird, but I still can't believe someone would intentionally make people ill."

"What do you know about Arthur Penrose?" Lily asked quietly.

Seren set her hands on her hips. "I know he's a sweet man who wouldn't hurt a fly."

"But all the information is here in his blog. Plus, he wrote a review for the restaurant saying he doesn't like people coming to the island and taking jobs. I think he's trying to scare off newcomers. Or sabotage their business in Dante's case."

"Not Arthur," Seren said. "There's no way in the world."

"You have to admit this is very suspicious," Lily said, holding the phone out again.

"Even if someone is intentionally poisoning people, everyone has access to the blog. And Arthur talks about it to anyone who'll listen. Someone could easily have got the information from him."

"That's true." Lily put the phone aside and inhaled deeply.

If it was Arthur who'd been sabotaging the food, he wasn't covering his tracks well.

But apparently he was someone who liked to talk, so hopefully he wouldn't be shy about answering a few questions.

Chapter Fourteen

As she left the pub, Lily called the garden centre to check when Arthur would be at work next. Sally didn't seem at all surprised by the question – not after Lily explained she wanted to take him up on his offer of advice about plants. She agreed he was the perfect person to talk to and told Lily he'd be working the following morning.

Once she got off the phone, Lily contemplated tracking Arthur down at home. She could usually find out where most people lived from Seren. But she wasn't sure going to his house was really warranted.

Unsure of the best course of action, she scrolled on her phone and hit dial on Flynn's number.

"I'm still at work," he told her. "We're sending samples from the baskets to the lab for testing, but it'll probably take a few days before we hear anything."

She rolled her eyes. "Not much point bothering then," she said, "I'll have figured it all out by then."

A gentle chuckle came down the phone.

"Is there anything new with Glynis?" she asked. "Did the hospital find out what's wrong with her?"

"I haven't heard anything."

"Did you find out much from the people who'd received baskets?"

"It looks like someone delivered them late on Friday night, but no one saw them being delivered."

The timing was useful at least, and she made a mental note to find out where Arthur Penrose had been on Friday evening.

"Have you found anything else?" he asked.

"Yes. The person who left the review for the restaurant is Arthur Penrose."

Flynn groaned. "Should I know who that is?"

"He works at the garden centre."

"Of course he does. You think he's poisoning people?"

Lily cut down a side street to the promenade. "I don't know but it seems suspicious."

"What do you know about him?"

"He's some sort of botany expert," Lily said as she arrived outside the ice cream shop. Impulsively, she crossed the promenade and wandered onto Porthcressa Beach. The wind caught her hair and pulled it behind her while her cheeks tingled with the warmth of the sun.

"He has a blog about plants," she went on. "One of his recent posts was about poisonous garden plants."

"That's a little disturbing," Flynn said. "Also a little stupid of him to publish a blog about poisonous plants if he was planning on poisoning people the same way."

"Yes." A smile pulled at Lily's lips. "But someone once told me that criminals often are stupid."

"Someone wise, no doubt." Flynn was smiling too – she could hear it in his voice.

"I don't know about that." She pulled a strand of hair from the corner of her mouth. "Anyway, Arthur's review of Dante's restaurant took issue with non-islanders moving here and taking jobs from locals. And then a bunch of newcomers were poisoned. That's probably not a coincidence, is it?"

"No, but again, I'd question why he's making no effort to cover his tracks."

"Maybe he doesn't even care about getting caught. Or thinks he's invincible or something." She turned into the wind and grinned widely. "Or maybe he doesn't think highly of the local police force and is confident they can't solve crimes, even if he leaves a bunch of clues."

"You're hilarious," he said flatly, but there was a hint of amusement in his voice.

"It does seem to be me who does all the investigative work around here."

"Because you're a private detective. I'm just a lowly police constable."

"Is Sergeant Proctor taking the poisonings seriously?"

"I imagine he will once I tell him what you've just told me."

"Maybe you shouldn't mention me by name. It might be better if you call me an anonymous source."

Flynn chuckled. "The sergeant's all right, really. I'll report back to him and see if he'll let me follow up."

"It seems a little unfair that I do all the work and you swoop in and take the credit."

"I wasn't planning on taking the credit." He went silent for a moment. "I have to get back to work."

"Do you think I should track Arthur Penrose down at home?" Lily asked quickly. "Or wait until he's at work tomorrow and question him there?"

"Definitely don't approach him in private."

"I was leaning that way too. But if he poisons anyone else in the meantime, you know I'll feel responsible."

"I mean it," he said sternly. "If you talk to him, you do it with other people around."

"Okay," she said, a hint of a whine in her voice. "Are you doing anything tonight?"

"No exciting plans," he said. "I thought I might come to your place and watch a film or something."

She grinned. "That sounds very exciting to me!"

"Do you feel like cooking, or shall I bring something?"

"I'll rustle something up," she told him and ended the call feeling energised.

Hurrying off the beach, she strode purposefully back to the shop. She'd make a couple of new batches of ice cream, then she'd figure out what to make for dinner. She also wanted to delve more deeply into Arthur's blog.

The afternoon went by in a blink and she felt a little flustered when Flynn arrived.

"I've only just started on dinner," she said as he followed her into the steam-filled kitchen.

"It smells great." He inhaled deeply. "What are we having?"

"Sweet and sour chicken with rice. The kind where the sauce comes from a jar, because I lost track of time and needed something quick."

"Sounds good to me. What have you been doing all afternoon?"

"I made a few batches of ice cream. Then I got caught up in Arthur's blog. It's kind of fascinating. He certainly does his research." She nodded to the table where her notes were laid out beside her laptop. "As far as I can tell, all the symptoms of the people who got ill could be attributed to some common garden plants."

"How do you know everyone's symptoms?"

"I don't, but there's a lot of chatter about it on social

media. I took as much info as I could from there." She jabbed at the open notebook. "My symptoms would fit with daffodils, but that just sounds pathetic, doesn't it?"

Smiling, Flynn flicked through her notes. "I asked the sergeant about Arthur Penrose."

"And?" Lily moved to the stove and pushed the chicken around the pan with a spatula.

"He wouldn't even entertain the idea that Arthur would poison people. Apparently, he knows him well and has a very high opinion of him. He seemed quite put out by the suggestion that he had anything to do with it."

"Even after you told him about the blog and the review?"

"Yeah. He says Arthur is harmless, and he sounded quite protective of him."

Lily wiped her hair from her forehead. "Seren was the same when I spoke to her about him."

"How old is he, by the way? Because the sergeant talked about him almost as though he was a child."

"I guess he's around thirty," Lily said. "But he comes across as quite childlike." Her mind drifted, thinking of the way Sally had also talked to him in a somewhat condescending way.

"I'm under strict instructions not to question him," Flynn said.

She glanced over her shoulder. "Thankfully, I have no one telling me who I can and can't talk to."

"Are you going to the garden centre tomorrow, by any chance?"

"I need plants," she said innocently.

Chapter Fifteen

USUALLY, Lily employed a covert approach to her investigations, but sometimes directness was needed. Given that Arthur Penrose didn't seem to be making any attempts to hide anything, it made sense to be upfront with him.

When she arrived at the garden centre the following morning, she found him wiping down the counter in the cafe.

"Hello!" he said cheerfully. "Sally said you might be here today. Would you like me to give you a tour and tell you about the plants?"

"I would like to talk to you about plants, but I don't need a tour. Do you have time to chat?"

He nodded eagerly. "Would you like a drink?"

She opened her mouth to ask for a coffee but clamped her jaw shut again quick as her stomach protested to consuming anything from the garden centre cafe.

"I'm fine, thanks," she said and moved to the nearest table.

"What can I help you with?" Arthur asked, his body altogether too large for the chair he lowered himself onto. "Is it houseplants that you're after?"

"I actually just wanted to ask you some general questions about plants." She smiled sweetly. "I saw you have a blog."

He tilted his head and looked faintly amused. "Who told you that? It's supposed to be a secret."

"I found it fascinating," Lily said, hoping a bit of flattery would put him at ease.

"Thank you. I enjoy working on it, and people tell me they enjoy reading the posts."

"I'm sure they do. The thing is, I saw you'd written quite a lot about poisonous plants..."

"Fascinating, isn't it?" He jutted his chin out. "Do you know what amazes me? So many plants have both medicinal and harmful properties. The same plant that could save a life could also kill someone. Isn't nature incredible?"

"It is," Lily agreed quietly. "I don't know if you've heard, but there have been some cases of poisoning on the island?"

"Something in those welcome baskets?" He nodded sagely. "Everyone has been talking about it. I'm sure whoever gave out the gifts must feel awful. They tried to do a good deed and accidentally made people ill."

"I'm not sure it was an accident," Lily said.

Arthur frowned. "I heard that some of the food in the baskets was out of date, or had gone bad or something?"

"No one knows for sure what happened. But it's a possibility that someone intentionally poisoned people." She waited for him to figure out that she suspected him, but he just stared blankly at the tabletop.

"Who would do something like that?" he asked.

"That's what I'd like to find out. I noticed in your blog posts that you listed a lot of the plants which could bring on the sort of symptoms the recipients of the baskets had."

"What kinds of symptoms?" Arthur asked.

"Stomach issues, headaches, dizziness..."

"I just assumed the food in the basket had gone bad," Arthur mused. "But if someone wanted to poison people, it can easily be done using plants."

"How would someone go about it?" Lily probed.

"Chop the plant up and add it to the food," he said with a shrug. "Or add some poisonous berries to the food... it really wouldn't be difficult."

"What about tea?" Lily asked. "Could you make a tea which makes people ill?"

"Of course. Dry out the plant and grind it up. Add it to some herbs to cover the flavour, and bob's your uncle, as they say." His brow furrowed as he looked at Lily.

"The same could be done with seasoning," Lily mused. "Like a bag of mixed herbs..." Just like in the welcome baskets.

Arthur nodded. "I don't know why anyone would do that, though."

"The recipients of the baskets were all newcomers to the island. The theory is that someone has an issue with people moving to the islands and taking job opportunities away from people who've been here for longer."

"Oh, yes." Arthur did his slow nodding again. "I've heard people talking about that."

"You said it yourself, didn't you? That you don't like newcomers taking the jobs?"

"No." His lips pulled downwards. "I like it when new people come to the islands."

"What about this review..." Lily unlocked her phone and brought up the review for the restaurant. "I believe you wrote this?"

His eyes brightened. "Yes. I wrote that review. We had a lovely meal. Dante's a very nice man."

"Then why did you write a review stating that you don't like newcomers taking jobs on the islands?"

"I didn't." Arthur pointed at the screen. "I just wrote that it happens, not that I don't like it."

Lily stared at him for a moment, trying to figure out if he was genuine or if he was playing games. His features were entirely earnest. Lily read the review again. He was right – he hadn't stated an opinion. It was implied that newcomers taking jobs was a negative, but it wasn't explicit.

It took Lily a moment to collect her thoughts. "Could I ask where you were on Friday evening?"

"Don't answer that, Arthur." The low voice rumbled directly behind Lily and she whipped around, startled.

"Hello, Denzel," Arthur said cheerfully. "I didn't know you were coming in today."

"Just need to pick something up for a client," he said, his gaze fixed on Lily.

If Arthur registered the icy atmosphere, he didn't react to it.

"Lily's been asking me about my blog."

"So I heard." Denzel's gaze softened as his attention shifted to Arthur. "You know you don't have to answer her questions. She's not the police. She can't come in here and start throwing baseless accusations around."

"She wasn't," Arthur said, a bemused smile stretching his lips into a thin line. "She was just asking how plants could poison people."

"She's asking because she's trying to figure out who did it. Even though it was probably an accident. Some people just enjoy stirring up trouble for their own entertainment."

Lily opened her mouth to respond but was interrupted by Sally crossing the room.

"What's going on?" she asked, glaring at Denzel. "Why the raised voice?"

"Because Little Miss Marple here has put two and two together and decided Arthur is poisoning people."

"What?" Sally asked, features scrunching up.

"You've no right to come in here harassing Arthur," Denzel growled at Lily.

"I wasn't harassing him," she snapped, finally able to get a word in. "I'm concerned that something sinister is going on, and I'm making enquiries to try to get to the bottom of it."

Sally's eyebrows rose dramatically. "You think whoever sent the baskets was *intending* to make people ill? I thought it was just an honest mistake."

"I suspect it was intentional." Lily looked from Sally to Denzel, deciding not to divulge her reasons yet. "But I'm not accusing anyone. I'm only asking a few questions and trying to figure out what happened."

"You're not the police," Denzel said harshly. "You're just some jumped up busybody who has no right to ask these kinds of questions."

"What questions?" Sally demanded.

Arthur cleared his throat. "Lily was asking where I was on Friday evening."

"When the baskets were delivered," Denzel said to Sally. "It's ridiculous, isn't it?"

"Not really." Sally pursed her lips. "It is odd that they were delivered anonymously." She shrugged and lowered her gaze to Lily. "I don't mind saying where I was. I had dinner at home with my dad, then we watched a bit of TV and I went up to bed about ten."

"I was at home all evening," Arthur said. "Doing research for my blog. And I watched a documentary about seals. Which was fascinating, actually."

"Do you live alone?" Lily asked him.

"Yes. My mum died four years ago. I've been on my own since then."

"Sorry," Lily muttered, feeling a pang of sadness for him.

"Leave him alone," Denzel said. "Arthur didn't do anything."

"I haven't said that he did." Anger coursed through Lily as she met Denzel's steely gaze. "Would you like to share where you were on Friday evening?"

"Not really, no." Denzel shook his head. "I don't have to answer to you."

"Oh, don't be silly," Sally said, her tone stern but affectionate. "None of us has anything to hide. Just tell her where you were."

His cheek twitched as though he might argue further before thinking better of it. "Fine," he said and shifted his weight. "I was in the pub."

"All evening?" Lily asked, more to annoy him than anything.

"All evening," he said through gritted teeth.

Lily forced a smile. "Thank you for your cooperation."

Chapter Sixteen

DURING A FIVE-MILE RUN with Flynn the following morning, Lily went over everything she knew about the poisonings. He was a good sounding board, but after chewing it all over, she still felt as though she'd hit a wall. The garden centre was at the heart of it all. That much she was certain of.

After a shower and a late breakfast, she answered the phone to Dante and spent fifteen minutes listening to him talk her ear off about his frustrations about the restaurant's lack of business. She attempted to reassure him that she was looking into things and would let him know when she had something concrete to tell him. When she finally managed to get him off the phone, she fired off a message to Maria, checking how she was.

It took half an hour for a reply to come. She said she was feeling better physically but was worried about Glynis. Lily's heart rate increased as her eyes flicked over the message which went on to say that Glynis had been airlifted to the hospital on the mainland earlier that morning.

Immediately, she hit dial on Maria's number.

"Is she okay?" Lily demanded as soon as she heard Maria's voice.

"The doctor insisted it's a precaution. She isn't happy with Glynis's progress and wanted her to have access to more specialist care if she needs it." She let out a frustrated sigh. "I don't really know how bad it is since I wasn't able to see her. I feel as though I've abandoned her."

"You can't help being ill." Lily swallowed hard, searching for something positive to say. "Glynis will probably see it as an adventure – a helicopter ride and a bunch of medical professionals to charm. She'll come back full of stories."

"Thanks," Maria said, apparently spotting Lily's attempt to cheer her up.

"I need to find out who did this," Lily said with a sudden feeling of urgency and a pang of guilt over sharing the smoothie with Glynis. "I'm going to look into this further," she said. "I'll let you know if I find anything."

"Good luck," Maria said quietly.

Tucking her phone away, Lily made a dash for the door. She wanted to speak to Arthur Penrose again, but she'd rather not do it at the garden centre this time, which meant she needed to track down his address. If Seren wasn't working at the pub, Noah Treneary would probably be there. He worked there too and was usually as good a source of information as Seren.

She didn't even make it as far as the pub before bumping into a member of the Treneary family. Kit was wandering along the promenade when she stepped outside – no doubt heading out to take a tour group around the island on his electric train.

"Hey!" he called, slowing as he approached her. "How are the preparations coming for the grand opening?"

"Oh." She glanced at the shop over her shoulder. That was probably what she should focus on. Still, there was time for that later. "It's all fine," she said limply.

"Are you okay?" Kit asked, tilting his head.

"Yes. I just heard that Glynis has been taken to hospital on the mainland and my head is a bit all over the place."

"Seren told me she was ill." His eyes were full of concern. "She also mentioned that you think someone is deliberately poisoning people."

She nodded sadly. "Do you know Arthur Penrose?"

"Yeah. Everyone around here knows Arthur."

"He recently posted on his blog about poisonous plants that are commonly found in gardens."

"Seren mentioned that too. It's quite the coincidence, isn't it?"

"Yes." Lily straightened her spine, happy that she wasn't the only one to think so. "Do you think he could have done it? He lives alone, and he seems a little odd…"

"No." Kit cut her off. "No chance. And he's not odd. He's a little different, that's all."

"Sorry, I didn't mean to sound harsh." She was surprised by Kit's defensiveness. "You did just say it's a weird coincidence that he wrote a blog and then people started getting poisoned."

"Yes, but I was thinking that someone read his blog and got ideas."

"Oh. I guess that makes sense." Except she had a funny feeling about Arthur. "Do you know where he lives?"

"Yes," Kit said warily.

"I only want to ask him a few questions," Lily insisted. "See if he can help me out."

He hesitated for a moment. "Give me your phone." Lily

opened the map app and passed it over. "Don't harass him," Kit warned as he handed the phone back with a pin dropped on the map. "If I hear you've upset him, we'll have a problem. Okay?"

A smile automatically lifted Lily's lips but fell away when she realised Kit wasn't joking.

"I won't upset him," she promised. "I'll just nip over and see if he can help me figure out who's been poisoning people."

"He'll be at the garden centre this morning," Kit said, checking his watch. "And this afternoon he'll be going over to Tresco. He helps in the gardens over there twice a week." He smiled gently. "Arthur is a man of routine. He only ever changes his plans if the weather is bad."

"The weather?" Lily asked.

"If the weather is bad, he won't get the boat to Tresco. That's the only thing that interferes with his routines." Kit backed away. "I have to get to the train." He raised a hand to wave before continuing on his way.

Alone, Lily stared at her phone screen. Apparently, if she wanted to catch Arthur at home, she'd need to wait until the evening.

But maybe he didn't need to be at home for her to do more investigating.

As she set off along the promenade, she called Flynn. He answered almost immediately.

"Missing me already?" he asked.

"Something like that," she said, rolling her eyes. "Have you got any plans for this afternoon?"

"Nothing exciting. What are you up to?"

"I'm on a little reconnaissance mission and thought you might like to join me."

"Does this involve any illegal activity?"

"Possibly a bit of trespassing, but only in someone's garden. You can sit that bit out if it's a problem for you."

"Who are you spying on?"

"I'll be at your place in a few minutes. Get your shoes on and come down. I'll tell you on the way."

Chapter Seventeen

TWENTY MINUTES LATER, they were standing at the front gate of Arthur Penrose's house. The property sat remotely in the northwest of the island, looking out to Tresco and Bryher and countless small islets. On a clear day, the view must be sensational, but everything was overcast today.

Unsurprisingly, the garden was perfectly maintained. Roses crept up the stonework at the front of the house on either side of the door. A neat lawn was intersected by a gravel path, which forked just beyond the front gate to lead to the front door and either side of the house.

"Knocking on someone's door isn't trespassing," Flynn said, turning the iron handle of the gate and pushing it open.

"He won't be home," Lily told him. "Apparently, his trips to Tresco are like clockwork."

"Well, we can knock on his door to see if he's home. If not, we could have a quick check to see if he's in the garden."

Lily grinned. "Can I also check to see if he's in his greenhouse?" She pointed at the glass structure to the left of the house.

"I think that would be fine." He lifted the brass knocker

and banged it three times against the door. "I guess he's not home," he said after a moment of silence.

"Funny that." Lily set off to the left. "Maybe he's in the greenhouse!" she said mockingly.

The gravel path crunched underfoot, breaking the silence. Lily's gaze swept over the plants in the beds along the dry stone wall which marked the edge of the property, but she couldn't pick out any she recognised from the blog.

Stepping beside her, Flynn peered through the glass panels of the greenhouse, then gave a small shake of his head and gestured to the door.

It screeched in complaint when Lily pulled the sliding door along its tracks.

"What are we looking for?" Flynn asked, stepping into the warm, humid air after her.

"I'm not sure." She walked along the centre aisle, between the potted plants at either side of her. "Something out of place, or maybe some of the plants listed on his blog. The poisonous ones."

"I'm no gardening expert but these look like baby tomatoes to me," Flynn said, pointing at the seedlings. "These are probably peppers, and I'd say these are sweet peas."

"You seem fairly knowledgeable," she said, a note of mocking to her tone since they were all clearly labelled.

A couple of orchids stood regally at the end of the greenhouse, along with a planter of leafy vegetables. Overhead, grapevines twisted. Nothing jumped out at Lily as sinister.

"I don't see anything interesting," she said, unable to keep the disappointment from her voice.

"Were you expecting him to have a selection of poisonous plants all neatly labelled?"

"No, but he also doesn't seem like the sort of person who would be too concerned with covering his tracks. I thought there might be some clues around here." She followed Flynn back outside and took a lungful of the crisp, fresh air.

Flynn looked back towards the lane. "We shouldn't hang around long."

"He won't be back for ages," Lily said, walking further around the side of the house. Her eyes lit up at the big, waxy green leaves around the back of the greenhouse. "That's rhubarb," she said, casting her eyes back to Flynn.

"And?"

"The leaves are poisonous if ingested. You'd need to eat a lot, but if you dried them and ground them up, you could add them to food and give someone nasty stomach problems."

"This is hardly evidence." Flynn stood beside her, staring down at the leafy plant. "Lots of people grow rhubarb."

"It's something." She turned on her heel and scanned the garden at the back of the house. "Lots of dandelions on the grass," she mused. "The leaves are also poisonous. There are daffodils under that tree, too."

"All of which can be found almost anywhere. It's hardly damning evidence."

"I suppose he'd keep any proper evidence hidden." She approached the window at the back of the house and cupped her hands against the pane to peer inside. Nothing shocking there, just a small living room with dated furniture and chintzy wallpaper.

"Let's go," Flynn said, tugging on her elbow.

"You didn't have to come," she said, clocking his serious expression.

"I probably shouldn't have. This feels dodgy now."

"Okay. We can go." As her gaze swept over the garden, she paused and lingered on the view beyond the border wall. The landscape shifted downwards on a gentle incline, and a narrow path led through grass and heather to a sweeping stretch of beach.

"Feel like taking the coastal route back?" she asked Flynn. "We could walk along the beach and find a path at the far end of it. Unless you're in a rush? The road will be quicker."

"I'm not in a rush," he said and changed course, heading for the wall at the end of the garden. With his long legs, he vaulted it effortlessly, while Lily took a little more effort to get over it.

They walked single file along the narrow path through gorse bursting with yellow flowers. Staying directly behind Flynn protected Lily from the wind until they were closer to the beach. Then the gusts grew stronger and seemed to come from all directions.

"Did you bring a raincoat?" Flynn asked, turning back to her.

"No. Why?"

He pointed to the mass of dark clouds out at sea. "I reckon we're going to get soaked."

"No." She wrinkled her nose. "It'll be fine."

"Yeah, right." He rolled his eyes. "You've brought me out in a storm."

"How was I supposed to know? The weather was fine when I set off."

He turned to continue on the sand-strewn path, which was bordered by rocks near the top of the beach. "The weather on this island is always so unpredictable. Sometimes it seems to change from one minute to the next."

Lily only faintly registered Flynn's words. Her gaze was fixed on a lone figure at the other end of the beach.

Grabbing at Flynn's arm made him stop at the same moment she did.

"What's wrong?" he asked.

She pointed. "I think that's Arthur."

"I thought you said he'd be out for the afternoon."

"He's supposed to be." Instinctively, she changed course, trampling over the dunes. "I guess the weather put him off going to Tresco."

"Where are we going?" Flynn asked, close behind her.

"I don't want him to see me." She slipped behind a patch of long marram grass and crouched low. "Get down!"

He did as he was told and Lily peered out, but had lost sight of Arthur.

"He's down there," Flynn said, pointing him out, strolling along by the waterline.

Lily grimaced. "I assumed he'd cut up onto the path. If he turns now, he'll see us." Without a lot of thought, she dropped to her bum and reclined onto the sand.

With an amused twinkle in his eyes, Flynn stretched out beside her and propped himself up on his elbow. "Lovely day for a bit of sunbathing."

"If I'm lying down, he won't see my face."

"Or he might be concerned that someone's collapsed and come to investigate," Flynn said, apparently finding her panic wholly entertaining. He had a point, though. They would look pretty weird lying in the sand when a storm was about to break.

"If he spots me, he'll know I've been snooping around. I don't want him to know I'm on to him."

"You seem pretty certain he has something to hide."

Lily braved a look down the beach, but dropped back again when Arthur turned in their direction.

"He could easily have put something in my smoothie," she said.

"This morning you said any of the staff could have done it.

You also mentioned that a staff member had been acting defensively when you were asking questions."

"Denzel? Yeah, he was shifty. He has an alibi, though. Arthur doesn't. At least not a verifiable one. What's he doing?" She didn't want to look again, so stayed flat on her back while Flynn peered around the grass.

"Heading this way." His lips twitched in amusement as he looked down at her. "It would have looked far less suspicious if we were just out for a walk on the beach and not hiding. This will look dodgy."

Annoyingly, he was right. Hiding in the sand dunes wouldn't be so easy to explain. Unless...

No, it was a stupid idea.

And Flynn would laugh at her.

It would explain them lying in the sand dunes though... and would probably deter Arthur from getting close enough to realise it was them.

"What's that look for?" Flynn asked, breaking her from her swirling thoughts.

She only hesitated for a moment.

"You should kiss me," she blurted out.

Chapter Eighteen

WITH HER HAIR splayed around her on the sand and her cheeks adorably rosy, Flynn's mind had been on kissing Lily from the moment he lay beside her. He hadn't expected her to give him the green light so explicitly, but he also wasn't about to waste the opportunity.

If he hesitated, she'd no doubt change her mind or insist it had been a joke or something.

Surprise widened her eyes as he shifted his weight so he was lying on top of her. His hand on her cheek had the effect of hiding her from view as well as tilting her face towards him.

He caught her sharp intake of breath just before their lips met in a kiss that made his pulse skitter. Their noses brushed together as he pulled back slightly, locking eyes with her.

Considering she'd told him to kiss her, she looked oddly confused by the situation. Presumably, she hadn't expected him to be so eager. Maybe he should have played it cool.

And maybe he should move away now.

He couldn't bring himself to. When he moved his lips back to hers, she reached a hand around his neck, pulling him closer.

His heart raced and his insides fluttered as he tilted his face and kissed her unrelentingly.

Somewhere, in the back of his mind, a voice told him to stop. They were friends and they shouldn't be kissing.

But they were, and it felt so bloody good that he couldn't bring himself to stop.

Eventually, he pulled back and forced his eyes open to face reality.

"What was that?" she whispered, her voice hoarse.

"You told me to kiss you," he said, not shifting his body from hers.

"I didn't think you'd just kiss me."

"I'm very obedient," he said cheekily.

"But..." Her throat bobbed as she swallowed hard. "I thought you'd ask why... Not just kiss me."

"I assumed it was to keep our faces hidden." Now seemed as a good a time as any to play it cool – better late than never. "And so it wouldn't look weird that we were lying in the sand."

"It was." Annoyance gave her words a bite. "But I thought you'd ask why before you kissed me."

"I've found it's best not to question it when women ask me to kiss them."

"I didn't want him to see me, that's all," she muttered. "It would be hard to explain what I was doing so close to his house, and I really don't want to make him suspicious. People get defensive if they know I'm on to them. It's harder to find things out."

"You could have just said you'd gone to his house to speak to him. I'm not sure he'd have assumed you went to his house to snoop."

"Well..." Her jaw tightened and her eyes flashed with irritation. "I didn't think of that."

"Clearly," he said, still not shifting away from her.

He *should* move, or he'd end up kissing her again. That probably wouldn't be a great idea. Not given the way she was scowling at him.

A large raindrop hit the back of his neck, encouraging him to move. Glancing around, he checked the coast was clear before sitting up.

"Arthur's gone," he said, after another quick glance along the beach. He got to his feet and offered his hand. "We should go. We're about to get drenched." His heart was still beating too fast and he was hyperaware of the softness of her skin as he pulled her up.

She stared at him, and he had the horrible feeling he'd just ruined their friendship. In all fairness, though, it was her who'd suggested he kiss her.

But she probably hadn't been expecting so much enthusiasm.

Which was surprising really, given the spark between them. He had a sinking feeling that the chemistry he'd felt might have been one-sided.

"We could jog," Lily suggested, dropping his hand and taking a step back. "Maybe we can get back before we get too wet."

"Maybe."

He didn't think so – not given the bloated drops that were falling from the sky at an increasing rate. Jogging sounded good though, since they wouldn't need to speak. Also, he felt the need to dispense some pent-up adrenaline.

They slipped into a gentle run along the sand and upped the tempo a little when they were on the solid path. As the rain fell harder, their pace intensified and by the time they took shelter in a shop doorway back in Hugh Town, they were both drenched and laughing as they fought to catch their breath.

"I'm not sure why we bothered to shelter," Lily said, her breathing levelling out. "I don't think I can get any wetter." She squeezed a strand of hair that was plastered to her face, causing a stream of water to fall from it.

Flynn looked down at his trainers. He raised onto the balls of his feet, then squelched back down. "I reckon you owe me a new pair of shoes."

She laughed, and her eyes lit up. "Why do you always make it sound as though I drag you places against your will? You could always say no. Or you could check the weather forecast."

"I lead a very sad life these days," he told her as they stepped back into the street, ducking their heads against the force of the driving rain. "Your little adventures keep me entertained."

Not only her adventures, but hanging out with her in general. Had he messed that up now? He didn't want their evenings in front of the TV to end because he'd stupidly kissed her. He didn't want their dinners to stop either, or the nights in the pub, and definitely not the ice cream tasting.

Should he mention the kiss? Or would that make it more awkward? The best thing was probably to pretend it had never happened. Just carry on as normal, and everything would continue to be normal between them.

When they reached the corner where they'd go their separate ways, she smiled at him in a way that didn't feel at all normal – it looked forced.

"I'll see you later," she said, the words almost a question.

He rubbed his hand over his wet hair, sending drips everywhere. "If you're refusing to compensate me for the shoes, you must owe me dinner, at least."

"I can manage dinner," she said.

"I'll get warm and dry and come over later." He took a few steps away from her, not leaving space for her to argue. "Message me if you need me to bring anything."

He quickened his pace, bracing against the wind and rain and hoping he hadn't messed up their friendship.

And that their kiss wouldn't lodge itself in his brain and torture him forever.

He suspected that was one hope too many.

Chapter Nineteen

LILY'S THOUGHTS whirled while she got dry and put on fresh clothes. She was waiting for the kettle to boil when her mind took her back to kissing Flynn. Her stomach fluttered and she paced to the living room, cursing as she went. She shouldn't be getting butterflies thinking about Flynn. He was her friend. There was no way anything could happen between them.

When the kettle clicked she went back to the kitchen, but only stared at the wall. She really valued her friendship with Flynn and she didn't want to lose it. Getting butterflies at the thought of him wasn't good.

It was only a kiss, though. There was no need for anything to change between them.

She lifted the kettle, then immediately put it down again. Time with her own thoughts wasn't what she needed. Grabbing her boots and raincoat, she ventured back out into the rain.

The downpour had eased off and only a few drops flicked from her coat when she pushed her hood back and slid onto a bar stool in the Mermaid Inn.

"You look pensive," Seren remarked, wandering over to her.

"I need a beer," she said. "And I need you to listen to me rant."

"I can manage both of those." She popped the top off a bottle of lager and set it in front of Lily. "What's up?" she asked, then leaned on the bar when Lily beckoned her closer.

"Flynn kissed me," she whispered, then watched in amusement as Seren's eyebrows shot up.

"Are you serious?"

"Yes. We were on the beach and he kissed me and now I'm freaking out."

"He just kissed you? Out of the blue?"

Lily bobbed her head ambiguously. "Kind of."

"I don't know why I'm surprised. The chemistry between you two is insane, but you were adamant you were just friends." Her gaze pierced Lily's. "Anyway, tell me all the details. What happened? Was it really romantic?"

"Not entirely. We'd been snooping around Arthur Penrose's place and we ended up hiding in the sand dunes. I was worried we were going to get caught out so I told Flynn to kiss me..."

Seren's brow wrinkled. "That was a lot of information," she said. "But you *told him* to kiss you?"

"Yes."

"So it wasn't *completely* out of the blue?" Her words were laced with mocking as she eyed Lily with exasperation.

"I didn't think he'd do it," Lily said forcefully. "At least not without me explaining why I wanted him to kiss me."

"And why did you want him to kiss you?"

"Because Arthur was on the beach and I didn't want him to see me so close to his house, so we hid in the dunes. But that looks weird, doesn't it – two people randomly lying in the sand dunes when the weather is miserable."

"Ah," Seren said knowingly. "So if Arthur glanced over, he'd just see a couple having a bit of fun and not think anything of it?"

"Exactly. It also meant our faces would be a bit more hidden. But Flynn didn't let me explain any of this. I asked him to kiss me and he kissed me."

Seren nodded her head slowly. "I knew he fancied you. It's been weeks since I saw him chatting up random women in the pub."

"Has it?" Lily asked, then chastised herself for sounding so desperate. What did she care about his romantic exploits?

"I actually never see him in here alone any more. If he comes in, it's with you."

"Okay," Lily mused. "That only means he's being discreet." She couldn't let herself imagine it had anything to do with her.

Seren's eyes twinkled as she smiled. "How was the kiss?"

"Um…" Lily blew out a breath, trying to find the right words. "It was…"

Grinning, Seren pressed the back of her hand against Lily's cheek. "That good, was it? You've gone bright red."

Lily pushed her hand away. "It was good," she admitted.

"What happens now?" Seren asked.

"Nothing," Lily replied and felt like her entire body was deflating. "It was only for show."

"Are you sure?"

Lily swallowed hard. "Afterwards he just carried on as normal." She felt her jaw tighten. "It was such an amazing kiss. I didn't want it to stop and I really had the impression that he was enjoying it, too." She paused and sighed. To her, it really had felt special. But she also hadn't had a lot of physical contact with anyone recently, so maybe she was just deprived.

"What happened right after you kissed?" Seren asked eagerly.

Lily shrugged. "He glanced up to check the coast was clear, then hopped up as though nothing had happened. I felt as though my insides had liquidised and my brain had forgotten how to string a sentence together, but he was all calm and cool, as though it was an everyday occurrence."

"Maybe he was just playing it cool so things wouldn't be awkward."

"I don't think so. He asked me to hang out tonight like we always do."

"Maybe he's going to come over and kiss you again."

"No," Lily said, while her traitorous stomach erupted with a quiver of butterflies.

"But you want to kiss him again?"

"No," Lily said unconvincingly.

"Are you going to continue to try to convince me that you only see him as a friend?"

"I was never lying. Not to you, anyway. I may have been lying to myself. But we can't be more than friends, so it makes no difference how I feel about him."

"Why can't you?"

"Because he's Flynn the womaniser," Lily said with an eye roll.

"I bet he'd give up his womanising ways for you." Seren pursed her lips. "I suspect he already has."

Lily put her hands to her face, then pushed them up through her hair. "He'll be leaving in a few months, and he's also my best friend. I can't risk messing that up."

"Oof!" Seren slapped her hand over her heart. "That hurts."

"My best *male* friend," Lily said while her lips stretched into a grin.

"That's okay then," Seren said. "I still think you can't rule out a relationship with him just because he's your friend. It's also going to be difficult to hide your feelings when you spend so much time with him."

"I know, but he's not sticking around. Even if this wasn't an unrequited thing, it makes no sense to start something with him."

"My guess is it's not unrequited," Seren said, raising her chin and smiling at a young couple who walked in. She gave Lily's hand a squeeze and told her she'd be back in a minute.

"I have to go soon anyway," Lily said, as Seren walked away. "Flynn is coming to my place to hang out."

The thought made her undeniably jittery.

"How come you were snooping around Arthur's place?" Seren asked when she returned.

Lily grimaced. "I just wanted to have a little look around his garden."

"To see if he has any poisonous plants?" Seren set her hands on her hips and tilted her head.

"I didn't find anything incriminating," Lily said with a shrug.

"Of course you didn't. It's Arthur. Please can you strike him off your list of people to question about this? I promise you it was nothing to do with him."

"Okay," Lily said with a distinct lack of conviction. She wasn't like Dante – she couldn't exclude people from her investigation because they didn't seem like the sort. "I'm fairly sure it's someone who's involved with the garden centre. Do you know a guy called Denzel who works up there?"

"Denzel Harris?" Seren nodded. "You can cross him off

the list as well. He's friends with my dad. I've known him all my life and he's a good guy."

"He wasn't happy about me asking questions."

"What kind of questions?"

"Mostly he didn't like me asking where people were on Friday evening when the baskets were delivered."

"You asked him for an alibi?" Seren rolled her eyes. "I'm not surprised he wasn't thrilled about that."

"It's only a problem for people who have something to hide."

"Where was he?" Seren asked.

"In here all evening."

A muscle twitched in Seren's jaw. She reached for a cloth and set about wiping the beer pumps. "On Friday?" she asked without catching Lily's eye.

"Yeah. Were you working on Friday evening?"

Seren gave a quick nod.

"And was he in here?"

She swallowed hard. "Did he definitely say he was in here?"

Lily thought back. "He said he was at the pub. I assumed he meant here, but no, he didn't specify. Maybe he was at the Old Town Inn."

"Maybe," Seren murmured.

"What?" Lily asked. "Why do you look as though there's something you're not telling me?"

"It's nothing." She tossed the cloth aside and rubbed at her forehead. "It's only that Kit was in the Old Town Inn on Friday evening and he didn't mention seeing Denzel. He told me about everyone else he saw, and I think he'd have mentioned if he saw Denzel because things have been a bit weird between them lately... but it doesn't mean anything. Kit probably forgot to mention it. Or maybe Denzel meant a completely different pub."

"Are there other pubs on this island?"

"There are pubs on the off-islands," Seren said. "Maybe he was in one of them."

"Does he usually go on a boat trip for an evening in the pub?"

"Probably not," Seren admitted, "But that doesn't mean he didn't on Friday. He might have been meeting someone from one of the off islands. He's good friends with John over on Tresco. They could have gone to the New Inn over there."

"You'd think he would have mentioned that," Lily mused.

"He could also have got the days mixed up," Seren said firmly. "There are lots of other conclusions we could reach before you write him off as a criminal. Denzel wouldn't hurt anyone."

"I'm going to check with Kit if he saw him in the pub," Lily said, getting her phone out. He replied immediately and they had a brief exchange.

"What did he say?" Seren asked once Lily put her phone away again.

"Denzel wasn't in the Old Town Inn."

"I'm telling you, that means nothing."

"You didn't see how annoyed he got with me for asking where he was," Lily said. "I'm pretty sure he lied to my face."

"That still doesn't mean he's done anything wrong."

"Maybe not," Lily said. "But it means I have more questions for him."

Seren sighed loudly. "You're kind of annoying when you're in investigator mode."

"Sorry," Lily said. "But someone poisoned people. And they tried to poison me too. I need to find out who it was."

Chapter Twenty

By THE TIME he left Lily's place that evening, Flynn was pretty sure he'd messed things up between them. On the surface, things were relatively normal. She'd prattled on about Arthur Penrose and Denzel Harris and her theories about the poisonings, then moved on to chatter away about the ice cream shop. It wasn't as though it was anything new for her to talk a lot, but there was a nervous energy to her wittering now – as though she didn't want to deal with any lull in conversation.

Even lounging on the couch to watch TV with her had felt odd. There was a tension in the atmosphere which he wasn't sure how to get past. With any luck, it would just take time and they'd slip back into their carefree friendship.

Thankfully, he was working first thing the following morning so he could focus on that and avoid dwelling on things with Lily.

"Did you hear from the lab about the stuff in the welcome baskets?" he asked Sergeant Proctor when he arrived at the station and wandered into his boss's office.

"No." He looked over his computer screen at Flynn. "I did

have a conversation with Dr Redwood yesterday. She's in touch with the hospital on the mainland and there's no change with Glynis Ward, but they've ruled out a virus or infection so she thinks it's most likely food poisoning. I'd already sent her the articles Arthur Penrose had written about poisonous plants. She agreed that if someone was intentionally trying to make people ill, the blog post would be a good resource."

"So someone really could have used common plants to poison people?"

"It's possible." He tilted his head. "Still seems far-fetched to me."

"Did you speak to Dante Accardi?"

"Yeah." He rubbed the bridge of his nose. "That guy can't half talk. Difficult to get a word in edgeways. As far as I can tell, there's no evidence anyone is out to get him. He sounds paranoid when he talks about it all."

"He only sounds paranoid if he's wrong," Flynn pointed out. "If he's right that someone is sabotaging his business, then he just sounds panicked and frustrated, which is entirely understandable."

"What else has your friend uncovered?" the sergeant asked wearily.

Flynn squinted in confusion. "Which friend?"

"How many friends have you got around here?" Sergeant Proctor asked with a twinkle of mischief in his eyes. "Your investigator friend. She's been nosing around, I take it?"

"Yes." He lifted an eyebrow. "Do you actually want to know what she's found?"

"Don't make me beg for information." He nodded to the chair and Flynn took a seat.

He proceeded to fill him in on Lily's theory that the garden centre was connected to the poisonings.

"No one at the garden centre would do anything like this,"

the sergeant finally said, leaning back in his chair. "Especially not Arthur. He's as gentle as they come." He dragged in a deep breath. "I know Sally Pengelly was looking for a job on the island a while back, so I suppose it makes sense for her to be frustrated with people coming to the island and taking jobs, but I really can't imagine her harming anyone. Maybe I'll go over there and have a chat with Gordon. See if anything feels off."

Flynn nodded and stood up. He paused in the doorway and looked back at his superior. "When we get the lab results back, you won't mind me sharing them with Lily, will you?"

"I can't imagine I could stop you," he said. "As long as she doesn't impede our investigations, I'm happy for information to be shared both ways. Providing there's nothing confidential."

"Of course," Flynn said. "Thanks."

As he moved out to take up position at the front desk, he automatically took his phone out, intent on messaging Lily to fill her in on the surprising conversation with the sergeant.

He paused, remembering that he'd kissed her yesterday and made things awkward. It didn't mean he couldn't message her.

After staring at his phone for a moment, he put it away.

He was still overthinking things when his shift ended. At his flat, he got changed out of his uniform and considered calling one of his mates in London. The situation with Lily would sound trivial though, and since none of his friends knew her, or anything about his life on the island, they just wouldn't get it.

These days, if he needed to talk to someone, it was always Lily, but this was hardly something he could chat to her about. As he pulled a T-shirt on, he had the fleeting idea of going to the Mermaid Inn to see if Seren was around. Except talking to her about it would be weird, and anything he said would likely get back to Lily.

It wasn't as though he didn't have friends on the island.

Maybe that wasn't true. The sergeant had probably been right when he implied Lily was his only friend. He had acquaintances, though, and some of them felt as though they could evolve to friendships.

Whenever he saw Jago Treneary, they always chatted easily. In fact, the last time he'd seen him, Jago had told him he should have a look at his brewery sometime.

It wasn't exactly a firm invitation and there was the chance he was only being polite, but Flynn was suddenly motivated to take him up on the offer of a tour.

Chapter Twenty One

FLYNN WAS ALMOST at Jago's place when he met Trystan and Kit Treneary walking the other way.

"If you're on your way to visit our brother," Kit said. "You should turn back now and save yourself from getting dragged into helping with his DIY projects."

Beside him, Trystan rolled his eyes. "I'm not sure you should complain, considering you spent the last two years dragging your brothers into your various renovation projects. Also, if Flynn helps Jago, that's less work for us to do."

"That's true." Kit grinned. "Carry on, it's great fun!"

"Thanks for the warning," Flynn said. "I'll take my chances. He has beer, right?"

"Yeah," Kit replied. "But he doesn't let you drink until you've worked for it. He's very mean."

Trystan gave his brother a friendly shove.

"Actually, he's not mean at all." Kit's eyes sparkled with amusement. "What I meant to say was that he has tons of beer and shares it willingly. You'll have a brilliant time!"

Flynn chuckled and lifted a hand in farewell as he left them. A few minutes later he was standing at the gate of what he thought was Jago's property. There was no signage, but he was sure he was at the right place. His gaze went to the house, then shifted to the bottom of the field where a large barn was located. Hammering started up, drawing his eye to a couple of people working on a wooden deck at the side of the barn.

He shouted a greeting, and the woman waved him over. Tramping through the slightly overgrown grass, he fought to remember the name of Jago's girlfriend. He was fairly sure it was Sylvie, but still found it an effort to keep track of all the members of the Treneary family.

"Hi," Sylvie said, grabbing his hand as soon as he reached them and depositing a handful of nails onto his palm. "It's so good to see you. You don't mind taking over, do you? He's not at all bossy. In fact, he's an absolute delight to work on DIY projects with."

Jago was on his hands and knees, hammering wooden boards into place, but straightened up, resting on his heels. "I only suggested that you could have the nails ready for me, so I don't have to ask every single time." He flashed Sylvie an affectionate mock-scowl.

"I'm going to make a start on dinner," she said and strode away.

"Hi," Jago said to Flynn. "You don't mind, do you?" He tipped his head at the nails in his hand. "I only have five more boards to do, then I'll give you a tour and we can have a beer."

"It's fine, just don't shout at me. You seem to have a reputation as something of a slave driver."

"You passed Trystan and Kit, I take it?"

Flynn nodded and handed over a nail.

"It's not so much that I'm grumpy about DIY..." He paused and gave the nail a few good whacks to drive it in. "It's that my family members are all a bit incompetent."

Flynn took a step and picked up the next plank for Jago.

"See!" Jago said. "Pass me a plank and then pass me some nails. It's not that complicated, but with them I have to politely ask them to pass me things every time."

"Politely?" Flynn asked.

"No." Jago wedged the board into place. "I wasn't polite at all in the end. And then they grumble, as though I'm the problem."

It didn't take much time at all until all the planks were in place. Jago stood and stretched, surveying his handiwork, before setting off to give Flynn a tour of his brewery in the converted barn. There was more than a hint of pride in Jago's voice as he outlined his plans.

The brewery had only been up and running for eighteen months, but he was already supplying most of the pubs and restaurants on the islands with his speciality brews, and would soon open the place up for tours and tastings. They'd have a little shop with merchandise too, and Flynn felt a jolt of envy as he listened to Jago talk so passionately about it all.

He'd never had any particular interest in being an entrepreneur, but if he were going to have his own business, it was exactly the sort of thing that would interest him.

After fifteen minutes of hearing all about it, they ambled towards the house, each with a bottle of beer in their hands.

"How's everything with you?" Jago asked.

"Fine." He slowed as they approached the patio at the back of the house and took a swig of his beer. "Something weird happened yesterday."

That was why he'd visited Jago – because he wanted someone to chat everything through with. It felt a little awkward to bring it up, but Jago knew Lily, and knew the relationship between the two of them.

"What happened?" he asked. "A work thing?"

"No."

Sylvie interrupted them, stepping out of the back door. "Do you want to stay for dinner?" she asked Flynn. "I'm making fajitas."

"If you're sure it's okay, I'd love to."

She smiled warmly. "It's fine with us. Shall we eat out here?"

Jago nodded in response. "Do you need any help?"

"It's all under control. You two chill out. It won't take long."

"Thanks," Jago called when she stepped through the patio door into the kitchen.

"Have you two been together long?" Flynn asked as they took a seat at the long wooden table.

Jago swigged his beer. "Not really. I met her when I came to visit for Trystan's wedding about eighteen months ago. Sylvie was visiting, looking for Lowen."

Flynn quirked an eyebrow, knowing there was a story behind that. "He's her cousin, right?"

"Yes." Jago's lips twitched in amusement. "Lowen has a different biological mother to the rest of us. Sylvie is from that side of his family. She's not *my* cousin." He stretched his legs out in front of him. "Anyway, we were both on the island for a visit and..." He shrugged, apparently deciding to keep the story short. "Now, here we are."

"So you weren't even living here then?" Flynn asked.

"No. I was living in New York, and had planned to move to London." His eyes roamed over the stretch of grass that led to the barn at the corner of the property. "Things worked out pretty well."

Flynn's thoughts flicked to his life in London and how much of a wrench it had been to move to St Mary's. For the first few weeks on the island, he'd been so bitter about the whole thing and was sure he'd hate every moment of his time here.

Now, when he thought about London, it was without the longing that he'd felt before. Over the last month or so, his anger had dissipated, and he'd stopped hating his time on the island.

He didn't love it, but he didn't hate it either.

"What was the weird thing that happened yesterday?" Jago asked, snapping Flynn from his thoughts.

"I kissed Lily," he said, deciding there was no point in beating around the bush.

Jago's lips pulled into a smirk. "That was pretty inevitable, wasn't it? You two seem very close."

"We are close, but just as friends."

"The fact that you kissed her suggests there might be something more than friendship."

Flynn shrugged. "We were investigating the poisonings, and we had to hide. The kiss was just a cover."

"Of course," Jago said, his voice ringing with amusement. "Seems totally plausible. So you're not attracted to her?"

"I didn't say that." He raised an eyebrow. "She's really cool, and she's very attractive. In other circumstances, maybe there could be something more between us, but I'll be leaving the island in a few months. We can only really be friends."

"Friends who roll around in sand dunes together?" Jago asked, grinning.

Flynn's eyes widened. "When did I say anything about sand dunes?" He stared at Jago, who continued his incessant grinning. "Did you already know about this?"

"I may have heard something. It's a small island."

"You can't be serious! Who told you?"

"I read about it in our family WhatsApp group."

Flynn's eyes felt as though they might exit their sockets. "What?"

Jago laughed. "I believe Lily told Seren who told Kit, and Kit wrote it on the group."

"Are you serious? Your entire family knows?"

He pursed his lips. "I'm not sure which group he wrote in."

"How many groups are there?"

"Far too many," Jago said, drawing his phone from his pocket. His eyes roamed the screen. "It was the one with just my brothers in it. But it doesn't make much difference. Everyone will have told their significant others." His features were filled with mirth. "There's a small chance Mum doesn't know. Assuming she hasn't seen any of the family this morning."

"And this is the sort of stuff you chat about in your WhatsApp groups?"

"Yeah. It's very sad, I know. But it's a small island. Not much going on."

Flynn tipped his head back and stared up at the darkening sky as he laughed. "This place is ridiculous."

"It really is," Jago agreed. "What's more ridiculous is how quickly you get caught up in the small-town gossip." He took another swig of his beer. "Was it a one-off then? The kiss?"

"I guess so. Like I said, I leave in a few months."

"You wouldn't consider staying longer?"

The question took Flynn by surprise. What was more surprising was that he didn't immediately baulk at the idea. He shook his head. "It's only a temporary position. I don't think I could extend even if I wanted to."

"Do you want to?"

"No," he said, but he didn't sound convincing even to

himself. "I have my flat in London and my job, my friends. I'm looking forward to getting back to it."

"A fling then?"

He screwed his face up. "What?"

"Would you have a fling with Lily?"

"No." He shook his head. "She's my friend."

"You keep saying that," Jago pointed out, amusement clear in his features.

"Yeah, but I mean, she's really my friend. How would I go from being friends with her to something else?"

Jago frowned. "Kissing her in the sand dunes seems like a pretty good first step. How were things afterwards?"

"I carried on as normal. I didn't want things to be awkward."

"Bad move," Jago said. "Things are supposed to be awkward while you transition out of friendship."

"It's turns out things are awkward, anyway. But I just told you I can only be friends with her."

"You're giving *me* mixed signals, so I imagine she's very confused. But if you're friends and you're attracted to her, I don't see why you wouldn't go for it."

"Because I'd like to stay friends with her."

"When I said have a fling, I didn't mean like a one-night stand. I just meant keep things casual and then see how things are when it gets closer to you leaving."

"It'll mess everything up," he said idly. "If I sleep with her, that's the friendship over."

Jago squinted. "When was the last time you were in a relationship?"

"I don't really do relationships." Flynn picked at the label on his beer. "Nothing long term, anyway."

"And by long term, you mean?"

"More than a few weeks."

"Wow." Jago stretched his legs out. "So it was always just sexual relationships?"

"Yep."

"Did you ever like any of these women?"

"Not especially, no."

"That's really sad."

Sylvie stepped out of the kitchen with a stack of plates. "It really is," she echoed, aiming a sly smile in Flynn's direction as she slid the plates onto the table.

"Great." Flynn groaned. "Is this conversation going to be circulated around your entire family?"

"No," Sylvie said. "You're safe talking to us. I'd say it's really Kit and Noah you have to be careful around."

"Keira can be gossipy too," Jago added. "Everyone else is fine. Lowen rarely passes information on even if you want him to."

"Come and help me bring the food out," Sylvie said to Jago, putting an end to the conversation about Flynn's love life.

Chapter Twenty-Two

EXERCISING HAD ALWAYS BEEN a solitary activity for Lily. At least until she'd moved to St. Mary's and fallen into the habit of jogging with Flynn. Now, it felt odd to set off for a run alone. She even felt a jolt of guilt for not inviting him when she stepped outside into the morning mist. She had her reasons, though, and it was nothing to do with the slightly strained atmosphere between them since they'd kissed.

It was that she was on a mission to engineer a meeting with Denzel and probe him about his alibi for Friday evening, which she was certain was fake. That was definitely a solo project.

If it weren't for that, she'd have invited Flynn along.

She was sure of it.

They hadn't been in touch at all the previous day, which was unusual, even though she knew he'd been working. It was probably more odd that they'd got into the habit of being in contact every day.

That's just what best friends did, though. It wasn't a sign that there was anything more between them. They'd both recently moved to the islands without knowing anyone, so it was natural that they'd gravitated towards each other.

With all her over-thinking, she almost ran right past the garden centre, but snapped out of her trance just in time.

Annoyingly, there was no sign of Denzel's truck in the car park. She didn't want to go inside, so she carried on running and looped back half an hour later to try her luck again. Still, there was no sign of him. She headed back towards Hugh Town and called in on Maria on her way.

Apparently, her previous manic behaviour really was down to sickness. Now that she was on the mend, she was aloof and kept Lily standing on the doorstep while they exchanged a few words.

She was feeling better, she said, and informed Lily that there was no change with Glynis. The doctors on the mainland were treating her symptoms and were hopeful she'd turn a corner soon. Maria promised she'd be in touch if she had any more news, then ended the conversation and retreated inside, closing the door firmly.

Maybe Lily had just got used to people on the island being friendly, but Maria's abruptness left her a little stunned.

As she set off again, walking this time, her mind drifted back to the way Maria had dragged Lily inside on her last visit, and how unnerving it had been when she'd talked about someone being out to get them.

They're not going to stop until we're dead.

The words rang in Lily's head. It had been a strange thing to say. Even if she thought someone was intentionally poisoning newcomers, there was no sign that anyone was trying to do more than warn people off.

Caught up in her thoughts, she almost missed Denzel walking out of the supermarket with a bag of shopping in his hand.

"Hey!" Lily called out, catching up to him at his truck. "I was hoping I'd bump into you."

"Yeah?" He opened the passenger door and put his shopping on the seat. The quirk of his eyebrow expressed more than a hint of disapproval. "What can I do for you now?"

"I just wanted to check... Which pub were you in on Friday night?"

He walked around to the driver's doors and pinned her with a frosty glare. "The Old Town Inn," he said, a rough edge to his voice. "Why do you want to know?"

"What time were you there?" she asked, ignoring his question.

"All evening," he muttered, clearly irritated. "I already told you that."

"The *entire* evening?"

"Yes." He opened the door to the truck. "I actually have a job to get to, if you've finished with your inquisition."

"So, just to be clear, on Friday evening you were in the Old Town Inn for the entire evening?"

"Yes! What the heck is your problem?"

"My problem is that someone tried to poison me. I'd like to know who it was. I'd also really love to know why you're lying about where you were on Friday night."

His knuckles turned white as he gripped the edge of the door. "What makes you think I'm lying?"

"Because Kit Treneary was in the Old Town Inn on Friday evening, and he said he didn't see you there."

Denzel slammed the door so hard that Lily startled and took an instinctive step backwards. "You've been talking to Kit Treneary about me?" he growled.

Lily squinted in confusion, because it didn't seem as though getting caught out bothered him as much as the fact that it was Kit who'd blown his alibi. She'd been dismissive when Kit had said Denzel was annoyed with him, but she was starting to suspect that Kit had it right.

"What's your problem with Kit?" she asked, tilting her head.

"I don't have a problem with Kit." Denzel took a deliberate breath, as though trying to calm his temper. "Look," he said evenly. "Maybe I got the days mixed up. It might not have been Friday that I was in the Old Town Inn."

"Where were you then?"

"At home, I guess."

"At home, alone?"

"Yes. The last I heard that wasn't a crime. Also, the last time I checked it was the police who were supposed to question people if they're suspected of a crime. I don't have to answer to you." He opened the door again, climbed into the driver's seat, and pulled away.

As she ambled home, Lily turned her phone in her hand, desperate to call Flynn and tell him about her encounter with Denzel. She wasn't sure if he was working, which annoyed her because usually he messaged her enough that she was aware of his schedule. Not knowing was a reminder that things weren't quite right between them.

She was almost home when the phone vibrated in her hand. In the second before her gaze hit the screen, she felt a pang of anticipation, assuming that Flynn had telepathically known she was thinking about him and been compelled to call.

Except it wasn't Flynn, and the disappointment she felt annoyed her immensely.

"Hello," she said, answering the call from Gordon Pengelly.

"Hi, Lily." His tone was clipped and business-like. "How are you?"

"Fine, thanks. And you?"

"Good," he muttered. "Listen, this is a bit of an odd phone call, but I thought it best to get things out in the open. I've just had a visit from Sergeant Proctor."

"Oh?" Lily said, a note of surprise in her voice that was entirely fake.

"Yes. We had a chat about a few things, mostly about those welcome baskets which I'm sure you've heard about."

Lily gave a hum of acknowledgement.

"He also had a few questions about the produce I've been supplying to Dante Accardi for his restaurant."

"Okay," Lily said, wondering when he was going to get to the point.

"Your name came up," he said, then cleared his throat.

"Really?" Lily asked, cursing the sergeant for bringing her into it.

"Yes. He said you've been looking into it. To be honest, I'd heard something about you being a private investigator, but I thought that was just a wild rumour."

"It's not an official thing," she said. "I just like to look into things sometimes. Especially when they impact me directly."

"And how do these supposed poisonings impact you?" he asked.

"I got a basket too." She hesitated, debating whether to mention the smoothie before deciding not to mention it for the time being. "I didn't eat anything from the basket, but a friend of mine received a basket and she got ill. They were all delivered to newcomers to the island, which definitely makes me nervous." As a thought occurred to her, she stopped dead. "I'm also opening a business, like Dante," she said, speaking her thoughts aloud. "I don't want my customers to get ill."

She felt vaguely ill herself at the thought of the products which had come from the garden centre. It'd just been fruits and herbs though, nothing dried like had been in the welcome baskets. She'd have noticed if they'd been tampered with. Wouldn't she?

"Ah, I see." Gordon's voice in her ear pulled her from her thoughts, but the subtle sense of unease stayed with her. "I'm sure you've got nothing to worry about. I can't imagine anyone around here is out to get anyone. The islands have always been a very welcoming place for visitors and newcomers."

"Good to know," Lily said quietly as she continued walking.

"Anyway, as well as the sergeant mentioning you, I also heard from Sally that you'd been questioning people here about their whereabouts at the time the baskets were delivered..."

He let the sentence hang in the air. Lily winced.

"Yes," she said slowly.

"You can't actually think one of my employees had anything to do with this?"

"At the moment, I don't know what to think. I'm just asking a few questions to see what comes up."

"I suppose that makes sense," he said reluctantly. "I imagine you'll find it's all a waste of your time, though."

She arrived in front of the shop. "How so?"

"I just can't imagine there's anything sinister going on. Sometimes food makes people ill, that doesn't mean it's intentional."

"Odd though, isn't it, that the baskets were delivered anonymously?"

"It was probably someone who wanted to do something nice but remain anonymous. Honestly, if it weren't for people getting ill, I'm sure no one would have thought anything about it."

"People did get ill though. If it was genuinely an accident, why wouldn't the person come forward and admit to it?"

"Would *you?*" he asked. "If you realised your good deed had made people ill?"

Lily inhaled a lungful of salty air. She wanted to say yes, she would come forward, but she wasn't sure it was true. It was hard to know since she couldn't imagine anonymously delivering welcome gifts to people she didn't know.

She ignored the question and changed tack. "If it turns out it was an accident, I'll be very happy." She'd also be incredibly surprised. "But I think it's better to err on the side of caution until we know for sure."

"I suppose you may have a point there. No harm in being vigilant to keep islanders safe. I'm just concerned that you may be unnerving people with yours questions."

Her mind flicked to Denzel slamming his car door, and she knew for a fact that her questions were ruffling feathers.

"I'll try to be more tactful with my questions," she said, her jaw tight as she lied. Tact wasn't her strong suit and sometimes being tactful was entirely over-rated.

"I'm glad we can talk so openly," Gordon said, before ending the call.

Lily opened the door to the shop and was halfway up the stairs to the flat when she fired off a message to Flynn telling him she'd had an interesting morning.

Relief flooded her when he immediately called her. She flopped onto the couch as she answered and proceeded to fill him in on the latest developments.

Chapter Twenty-Three

WHEN THE DOORBELL chimed early the next morning, Lily all but jumped off the couch. After her phone call with Flynn yesterday, she was hoping everything was back to normal between them. He was working today, so she wasn't sure if he would call in.

Peeking from the living room window to see if it was him, she was surprised by Mirren Treneary looking up. After raising a hand to indicate she was coming down, she slipped her trainers on and a thick cardigan.

"Sorry to call in so early," Mirren said when Lily opened the door. She didn't wait for an invitation before striding inside. "I needed to talk to you, and I didn't want to wait." When she reached the counter, she turned and scanned the shop before her eyes settled on Lily. "It's about Denzel Harris," she said, clasping her hands in front of her.

"Okay." Lily locked the front door and moved towards Mirren. "What about him?"

"He says you've been harassing him about this whole poison thing."

Lily's eyebrows shot up. "Harassing is a strong word. I asked him a few questions, that's all."

Mirren opened her mouth, then closed it again and inhaled deeply through her nose. "He's got nothing to do with the poisonings. You don't need to question him."

"He was very cagey when I asked him where he was on Friday night," Lily said slowly, unnerved by how jumpy Mirren seemed.

"That doesn't mean anything. Half the time I can't remember what I did the previous day, never mind a week ago."

"It wasn't just that he couldn't remember where he was," Lily said. "I'm fairly sure he was outright lying. And when I pulled him up on it, he got a little aggressive..."

"Aggressive in what way?"

Lily thought back on her confrontation with him. "Slamming the door and raising his voice, and just his overall demeanour."

"He's not an aggressive person," Mirren said, squeezing the bridge of her nose. "He must have been frustrated with your questions. I can promise you he didn't do anything."

"You can't really *know* that," Lily argued. "You've just said he's not an aggressive person, but that's not what I saw. So maybe you don't know him as well as you think you do."

Mirren glared at her. "I've known Denzel for over thirty years. I can tell you for a fact he's got nothing to do with this."

Lily gripped the back of the chair closest to her. "I'm sorry, but in my experience, you can never truly know someone. You think you know someone inside out, but they can always surprise you."

Immediately, Mirren's features softened. The tilt of her head expressed so much pity that Lily took a step back, as though she could avoid it.

"I'm sorry that's been your experience," Mirren said sadly. "But I've lived a lot longer than you and I promise it's not true. Find the right people and you can absolutely know them as well as you know yourself."

Lily shifted her weight, hating the turn of the conversation and the lump which had wedged itself in her throat. "I just don't see why Denzel was so cagey about where he was on Friday."

"Did it ever occur to you that he remembers exactly where he was, but he doesn't want to share that information with you? And not because he was doing something criminal."

"I'm not saying that's not a possibility, but..."

"Lily!" Mirren snapped, cutting her off. "He was with me, okay? He had dinner at my place. That's how I know he wasn't out delivering poisoned gifts on people's doorsteps."

"We don't know exactly what time the gifts were delivered, but it could have been late."

"It wasn't Denzel," Mirren said confidently.

Lily frowned, thinking back on how annoyed Denzel had been about her questions. "Why didn't he tell me he was at your place?"

Mirren let out a frustrated sigh. "For someone who fancies themselves as an investigator, you can be slow to catch on sometimes."

Lily's brain whirred for a moment. Then her eyes widened. She opened her mouth to speak, then paused and considered her words. "How late did he stay at your place?" she asked carefully.

"All night," Mirren said.

Lily felt her eyebrows rise. "Until the morning?"

"Yes. Are you getting the picture now?"

"I think so." She hesitated as the information sunk in. "And you're not just saying this to give him an alibi?"

"No!" Mirren laughed. "My kids don't know that he sometimes stays over. I don't want them to know yet. So if Denzel was snappy with you, it was because he was worried about covering for me, not for himself. He'd actually like my family to know about us."

Again, Lily pondered the information. "I guess he's pretty attractive for an older guy."

Mirren snorted. "Funny, because in my eyes, he's a younger guy."

"How old—" Lily stopped herself, not sure she knew Mirren well enough to delve into her private life.

"He's ten years younger than me," Mirren said, smiling lightly. "Could you please cross him off your list of suspects now?"

"Yes."

"Thank you." She took a deep breath. "Also, I know you spend time with Kit and Seren..."

"I won't say anything." She shook her head. "You realise your kids aren't actually kids any more? They're adults."

"I know that." She shifted the strap of her handbag on her shoulder. "They're grown men. But they're also just boys who miss their dad."

Lily nodded slowly. "They also love their mum, and from what I know of them, I think they'd just want you to be happy."

"You're right," she said. "I do plan on telling them. I just wanted to figure out how I felt myself first."

"You don't have to worry about me saying anything."

"I appreciate that. And I'm sorry that you got a poor impression of Denzel. He's a good man, really."

Lily nodded again and walked Mirren to the door.

Chapter Twenty-Four

By MID-MORNING LILY was putting the finishing touches to a large rectangle of blackboard paint on the back wall of the shop. The door opened, and she called *hello* to Kit and Seren, but neither of them greeted her. Kit lifted a finger to his lips in a shushing motion, then pressed the button on the side of his phone to increase the volume of the chatter coming through it.

"Is that Gordon Pengelly?" Lily whispered, sure she recognised the voice.

Seren nodded. "He's being interviewed on the radio. Mirren just messaged to tell us. We thought you'd want to listen too."

As Kit set his phone on the counter, Lily huddled around it with the two of them, tuning in to the conversation.

"It goes entirely against the ethos of the island," Gordon was saying in a slightly pompous tone. "We've always welcomed visitors to the island, whether it be day trippers or those who stay for longer."

"Come on," the interviewer said. "You have to admit there's often some rivalry between born and bred Scillonians and the people who move here."

"A *friendly* rivalry," Gordon said. "We're talking good-natured banter, nothing more."

"What radio station is this?" Lily asked.

"The Scillies have their own radio station," Kit replied.

"Wow," Lily muttered, not sure how she was only just finding that out.

"The islands need more business," Gordon continued. "It's good for our economy. But no business in the gastronomy sector can survive the backlash from making people ill. Dante Accardi was telling me he hasn't had a customer in weeks. Even though he's replaced all his food supplies, people just aren't willing to risk it. I know all of this is making Lily Larkin nervous, too."

Lily's eyebrows shot up at the sound of her name and she moved closer to the phone, waiting for him to go on.

"Ah," the interviewer said, a cheerful lilt in his voice. "Our very own private investigator. Why would she be worried?"

"She's a newcomer," Gordon said. "If something sinister is going on, that puts her at risk. She's also about to open an ice cream shop. Imagine if she's the next target for this saboteur."

"Surely not," the interviewer said. "You couldn't sabotage ice cream, could you?"

"I don't know," Gordon said. "But I know I'd be worried if I was her. I'm worried *for* her."

"With any luck she's putting her investigative skills to use to catch whoever's trying to drive newcomers away."

"I hope so," Gordon said. "We need to sort this out, and soon. Everyone on our islands should feel safe. What's been happening is entirely unacceptable. Until we get to the bottom of it, we need people to be careful."

There was a puzzled undertone to the interviewer's voice. "Are you saying people shouldn't eat out?"

"No." He sighed heavily. "We can't give in to fear, can we?" There was a brief pause. "I'm sorry. I really don't know what the answer is. Of course people are going to be nervous about eating out for a while. The police are working on the matter. I'm sure they'll have answers for us soon."

The interviewer thanked Gordon before introducing a song.

Lily looked up at Kit and Seren.

"*Are* you worried?" Seren asked, while Kit took his phone and turned the radio off.

"I am now," Lily said. "I mentioned to Gordon that I was concerned but he insisted I shouldn't worry. Apparently he changed his mind about that."

Seren grimaced. "You don't think someone would try and poison your ice cream?"

"I really hope not." Her heart was thundering at the thought of it.

"I suppose it's good that Gordon's spreading awareness," Kit said. "Everyone should be a bit more vigilant."

"There are articles in the press on the mainland too," Seren said.

"Why?" Lily asked. "Did the police put out a statement or something?"

"I don't know." Seren frowned. "I thought you might know."

Lily let out a sigh that was part growl as she pulled her phone out. "I'll ask Flynn."

Chapter Twenty-Five

Rather than responding to Lily's messages, Flynn wandered over to visit her on Wednesday morning. When he told the sergeant he was nipping out for a while, he didn't bat an eyelid. The atmosphere between the two of them had relaxed in the past few weeks. He'd even say that they rubbed along well.

"This looks like good timing," Flynn remarked when he walked into the shop to find Lily staring forlornly into a bowl of ice cream. "Do you need a taste tester?"

"No." She pulled the bowl closer to her.

He frowned, thinking things might be worse between them than he thought if she was no longer letting him taste the ice cream.

"What's going on?"

"I'm checking to see if it's poisoned."

Confused, he shook his head and pulled out a chair.

"I know what you're going to say – that I'm just looking for a reason to delay opening the shop, but that's not what's going on. I'm genuinely worried the ice cream is going to make people ill."

He frowned. "Because some of your ingredients came from the garden centre?"

"Yes. I washed everything well, but I didn't examine everything closely."

"The results came back from the lab," he told her solemnly. "In both the herbs and the tea they found compounds that were consistent with daffodils and hydrangeas."

"No way!" Lily slapped her palms on the tabletop, making him wince. "*Daffodils and hydrangeas?* I can't believe you're serious."

"You were the one who's been saying all along it was garden plants."

"I know, but hearing you say it sounds completely ridiculous. What a pathetic way to poison people." She stared down at the ice cream in front of her. "This is going to make me ill, isn't it?"

"It won't if you don't eat it." He felt his eyebrows pull together. "But there's no way anyone slipped dried herbs or tea into the ice cream is there?"

"No, but if they're taking advice from Arthur's blog they probably also know you can poison people with fresh leaves from the plants. What if the mint leaves weren't all mint leaves? What if there was another plant in there too?"

"Can you throw out everything that has ingredients from the garden centre and make it again?"

"I can, but that won't leave me with much ice cream. It's only a few days until the opening. I won't be able to get my hands on enough fresh supplies to make new batches before Saturday." She frowned as she put a spoonful of ice cream in her mouth.

"What the heck are you doing?" Flynn snapped, pulling

the bowl away from her. "Are you seriously trying to poison yourself?"

"I'm hoping it's not poisoned," she said sadly. "But this seems to be the only way to figure out if there's a problem with the ice cream. If I get ill, I'll know I can't serve it, and I'll have to postpone the opening. Or *maybe* I can make enough ice cream without the supplies from the garden centre, but I'm not sure I'd have enough. It would also leave me with fewer flavours, which would be disappointing."

He stared at her, trying to figure out if she was serious. "You can't eat it if there's a chance it's going to make you ill. If you think the food has been tampered with, that's a perfectly good reason to postpone the opening."

"No, it's not." She reached for the bowl, which he moved further out of her way. "It's one thing not to open because of my own stupid insecurities, but I refuse to let someone else scare me out of opening."

She held her hand out for the bowl of ice cream and he shook his head. "Postpone the opening," he said firmly.

"The most likely scenario here is that I get a nasty stomach ache. But maybe the food is fine. I don't want to throw everything out for nothing."

"This seems really stupid," he said, finally releasing the bowl.

Lily plunged her spoon into the ice cream. "What's stupid is that I didn't consider that there might be a problem with the ice cream earlier. I wouldn't accept a drink when I was up at the garden centre, but somehow it didn't occur to me to wonder if the food I took from them might be problematic." Gingerly, she put the spoon in her mouth. "If I'd thought about it, I'd have looked more carefully at the ingredients before I made the ice cream."

"I don't like this plan." He rubbed at the back of his neck

and remembered the message he'd received from her. "Why were you asking if we'd been talking to the press?"

"Because it's all over the news. Haven't you seen it?"

He shook his head and pulled out his phone to check his apps. "Not headline news," he told her when he struggled to find anything.

"Dig around a bit and you'll find it." She sighed. "If it didn't come from the police, I wonder who's been spreading the word. Did you hear Gordon's radio interview?"

"No," he replied, feeling entirely out of the loop.

"You can listen to it on replay." With a few taps on her phone, she set it playing for him, then took another spoonful of ice cream.

Watching her eat it pained Flynn.

"That's enough," he said, unable to concentrate on the interview while she ate the potentially poisoned ice cream.

"I should probably have a bit more."

He shook his head. "How much of the smoothie did you drink before you got ill?"

"Not a lot."

"That should be enough ice cream then," he said, moving it away from her.

With a sigh, she dropped the spoon into the bowl and they fell silent to listen to the radio interview.

"So that's what got you worried about the ice cream," he said when it came to an end.

Lily nodded.

"It's weird, isn't it?" she said after a moment. "Because he kind of sounds like a concerned citizen warning people to be vigilant. But..."

"He also sounds as though he's scaremongering," Flynn finished for her.

"Yeah."

"If you were trying to keep newcomers from coming to the islands, spreading the word that people are being poisoned seems like a good way to go about it."

Slowly, Lily nodded. "The interview definitely gave me bad vibes about Gordon."

"I'm surprised you're not already questioning him."

"I would be if I wasn't seriously questioning my judgement."

"In what way?"

"I thought it was Arthur, and then I decided it probably wasn't. And then I thought there was something fishy about Denzel but I turned out to be way off. Now I think Gordon is suspicious..."

"That's how investigating works," Flynn pointed out. "You check out everyone who seems suspicious until you land on the right person."

"Maybe, but I'm still questioning my judgement." She dropped her chin to her chest. "Not only because I feel as though I'm chasing my tail trying to figure this out, but also because I just consumed ice cream that I think might be laced with poisonous plants." She raised an eyebrow. "Overall, I'm questioning my choices."

"I'll admit that eating the ice cream seems like a bad call, but the rest of it is going well."

"I told you, I'm chasing my tail."

Flynn smiled as he leaned on the table. "The sergeant has been asking me for updates on your findings."

"That makes sense. He's concerned about who I'm going to upset next with my rogue investigations."

"No," Flynn said. "He wants to be kept updated because he thinks you get good information."

"No, he doesn't," Lily insisted.

"He does." Flynn grinned, endeared by her disbelief. "He

even said I'm allowed to share information with you, because we get such good information from you."

"Are you serious?"

Flynn leaned back in his seat, a warmth in his chest that he'd got the spark back in her eyes. "I doubt he'll admit it to your face, but I think he's pretty impressed by your work."

"He should be," she said, her self-confidence returning in a rush.

"You said you've crossed Denzel off your list of suspects?"

"Yeah. Turns out his alibi is airtight."

"I thought you said he was lying about his alibi?"

"He was, but now I know why and it puts him in the clear."

Flynn arched an eyebrow. "Should I ask?"

"No." She shook her head. "Sometimes I have to keep things confidential."

"Fair enough."

"Really?" She looked sceptical. "You're not curious?"

"I am curious, but I don't think it will kill me not to know."

She lifted a shoulder in a subtle shrug. "I'd tell you if I could."

"Okay." He smiled to reassure her that he didn't have a problem with her keeping things to herself.

Her phone buzzed on the table and she lifted it to read the message. "That seems like my cue to go and question Gordon."

"Who's the message from?"

"Dante. Wanting a progress report." She stood abruptly. "I'll go and question Gordon before I start vomiting from this ice cream."

"Shall I come?" he asked.

"No. Your uniform tends to scare people into silence."

164

That was fair enough. Also, Sergeant Proctor had already been to question Gordon and he didn't want to get into trouble for harassing him.

"Keep me updated," he told Lily.

"Will do."

"On your health as well as anything you find out from Gordon Pengelly!"

She grimaced and headed for the door.

Chapter Twenty Six

A FEW CUSTOMERS were strolling between the rows of plants when Lily arrived at the garden centre.

"Hello!" Arthur said, pausing his conversation with an older couple and raising a hand to wave at Lily. If he felt any animosity towards Lily after her questioning him, he was keeping it well hidden.

"Is Gordon around?" she called.

"He's not here," Arthur replied. "Sally's in the cafe, though."

"I'll say a quick hello to her." Hopefully, Gordon would be back soon.

Sally's face lit up when Lily walked into the cafe area. "I was just thinking about you," she said, with a sympathetic tilt of the head. "How are you?"

"Good, thanks."

So far, anyway. With any luck, the slight discomfort in her stomach was merely unease at the thought that she might just have eaten poisoned ice cream and not actually the first twinge of food poisoning.

Sally scurried out from behind the counter to place a

hand on Lily's shoulder. "How are you feeling about the opening of the ice cream shop?"

"A bit nervous," Lily confessed while her hand automatically went to her stomach.

Sally's smile was all sympathy. "Dad and I were talking about you last night. Saying how nerve-wracking it must be for you. Especially with all this talk about these poisonings." She shook her head. "Although, I have to say, I'm inclined to think it's all been blown out of proportion. It probably was just someone trying to do something kind and making an honest mistake."

"I'm afraid not," Lily said automatically. "The lab results show that there were compounds from garden plants in the products in the welcome baskets. The kind of plants which shouldn't be ingested."

Sally's eyebrows twitched. "It still could have been an honest mistake."

"I suppose if it was only the welcome baskets, that could be the case."

Sally frowned, then looked across the room as the only customers in the cafe got up to leave. She thanked them for coming and called out a cheerful goodbye.

"What do you mean?" she asked Lily, moving away from her and plucking a tray from behind the counter.

"Someone is trying to run Dante Accardi out of town." She caught the air of puzzlement in Sally's features as she went to the vacated table. "The Italian restaurant," Lily explained. "Dante believes someone has been sabotaging his food."

"Oh, that." Sally busied herself with loading mugs and plates onto the tray. "I'm sorry but I find it hard to believe someone has such a grudge against newcomers to the islands.

How would someone even go about sabotaging his restaurant?"

"He doesn't know," Lily said. "He asked me to look into it."

"Did you find anything?"

Lily chewed on the inside of her cheek, debating how much to say. "I found out that he gets some of his food supplies from here," she said quietly.

Sally stopped loading the tray and lifted her gaze to Lily. "So?"

"So it would be a convenient way for someone to sabotage his business."

"You think someone here has been poisoning people?" She huffed out a humourless laugh and picked up the tray.

"I'm looking into that theory, yes." Lily had to move quickly to keep up with Sally as she went back to the counter.

"I thought you were questioning Arthur because of his blog, not because you were suspicious of everyone who works here."

"Like I said, I'm just looking into the theory."

"You can look all you want," she said, rolling her eyes. "But it's ridiculous. Nobody here would do that."

"Can I ask you a question?" Lily said, trying to pin Sally with her gaze as she cleared the items from the tray into the dishwasher.

"What?" she asked impatiently.

"Were you upset when you couldn't find a job on the island?"

A muscle twitched in her jaw and Lily wasn't convinced she was going to answer. Finally, she stopped with her cleaning and turned to face Lily.

"No," she said evenly. "I wasn't."

"You must have been a bit disappointed."

She shook her head. "If I wanted a job here, I'd have found one."

"How do you mean?" Lily asked.

"I mean, I have a degree in accounting. If I wanted to stay on St Mary's, I could set up my own business. I'd find a few clients locally, and some more who I could work for remotely." She threw her hands up. "I could also work *here,* if it was just about earning enough to live on the island."

"I don't understand," Lily said. "I thought you'd been job hunting."

"I had a half-hearted job hunt," she said with a sigh. "But it was only really for my dad's benefit. I want to live on the mainland. I went to university in Bristol and I loved it. My heart is there, not here. But I know that's hard for my dad to accept, so for a while I pretended to be checking out my options. Just to give him time to get used to the idea of me living in Bristol permanently."

Lily's mouth hung open as she considered the new information. "So you were never upset about the job situation here?"

"No." She wrinkled her nose. "What did you think, that I might be poisoning newcomers to keep the Scillies strictly a place for true Scillonians?"

"I think it's a reasonable motive."

"It's crazy, and it doesn't even make sense. Most of the businesses here rely on visitors."

"Visitors, yes. But people who move here and set up home, and open businesses or take jobs?"

"Everyone is welcome," Sally said. "I know there can be some banter between born and bred Scillonians and people who move here, but it's only fun. No one means anything by it."

"Your dad must have been upset about you not finding a job over here," Lily said.

Sally slapped a hand on her forehead. "Now you're going to accuse Dad!" She rolled her eyes. "I can certainly see why Denzel was upset with all your questions. Your crazy accusations are quite offensive."

"People have been poisoned," Lily pointed out. "Glynis Ward is still in hospital. I only want to make sure it doesn't happen again."

"My dad is one of the most caring people I know," Sally said fiercely. "Did you hear him on the radio this morning? He's concerned about the residents, and doing everything he can to make sure people stay safe."

"Is he?" Lily asked. "Or is he creating a panic which will deter people from moving to the Scillies?"

"You sound insane," Sally said, eyes flashing with anger. "I think it would be better if you leave. And given what you're insinuating, I'm not sure it's going to work out for us to continue to supply you with produce for your ice cream."

"Okay," Lily said, backing up. She might have gone too far, but she also knew that her investigations would always make people ill at ease.

She suspected that the more uneasy people were with her questions, the closer she was getting to the truth.

Chapter Twenty Seven

Out in the car park, Denzel hauled bags of soil from a trolley into the back of his truck. Directly in Lily's path, it would be awkward to ignore him. Not that she wanted to. While she felt as though she was turning people against her at every turn, she could at least clear the air with him.

"Hi," she said, stopping beside the trolley.

He gave her a cursory glance and tipped his chin, but didn't pause in loading his truck.

"Mirren explained everything," Lily said, filling the uncomfortable silence.

Again, he only acknowledged her with a quick flick of his chin.

She wasn't sure what else to say. She could apologise, but she wasn't convinced she owed him an apology.

"Okay, then," she muttered as she set off again.

She was all the way to the other side of the car park when the crunch of tyres on gravel made her stop and turn.

Denzel's window rolled down as he slowed beside her. "Need a lift?" he asked.

Suspicion swept up Lily's spine, and she glanced around while she stalled for a reply.

"I was stressed the other day," he said, rubbing at his jaw. "Which is no excuse – I shouldn't have taken it out on you." He caught her eye and lifted an eyebrow. "I'm sorry."

"Okay," Lily said, nodding her acceptance.

"Do you want a lift home?"

She shrugged before deciding she didn't need yet another trek across the island.

"Kit thinks he's done something to offend you," she stated bluntly, while she pulled the seatbelt around her.

"What?" His features crinkled in concern as he looked across at her. "Why?"

"Because when he invites you over to his place, you make excuses."

He pulled out onto the road and kept his eyes fixed ahead for a moment. "I make excuses because I'm in a relationship with his mother and he doesn't know. It's a little uncomfortable."

Lily nodded. "He thinks you just got fed up with him asking for help with his DIY projects."

"I enjoy helping him with his renovations." A muscle twitched in his jaw.

"Maybe you should tell him that."

He leaned onto the steering wheel. "I can't. Not until Mirren tells them what's going on between us. Every time I see Kit, or his brothers, I feel deceitful. I've known them since they were kids and this whole situation feels extremely awkward." He slowed at a junction and glanced up and down the road before pulling away again. "Which is why I got so het up when you were quizzing me."

"I can see that now."

"It wasn't only that." He cast her a sidelong glance. "I was also annoyed with you for questioning Arthur."

"Nobody seems to like me questioning Arthur," she said with a sigh.

"Because everyone knows he would never hurt anyone. And he only ever sees the best in people. Which means that even when you question him, he thinks you're his sweet new friend and wants to help you."

"I am very sweet," Lily said, smirking. "And if everyone went out of their way to help me, my investigations would go much more smoothly."

"I'm sure," Denzel said. "But I would appreciate it if you'd back off Arthur."

"I haven't entirely written him off my list of suspects, but he's also not top of my list any more."

"Am I still on your list?" Denzel asked as he manoeuvred through the streets of Hugh Town.

"No. You're off it. You can thank Mirren for that."

Lily caught his flash of a smile at the mention of Mirren, but it was gone again in an instant.

"You really believe someone is intentionally poisoning people?" he asked, pulling up to the curb on the road that ran behind the promenade.

"Yeah. I do." She reached for the door handle.

"Hang on a sec," he said, then cleared his throat.

Lily looked at him quizzically.

"I wanted to ask you something..." He trailed off, looking thoughtful. "Actually, it doesn't matter. Never mind."

Her insatiable curiosity meant Lily didn't move an inch, but tilted her head while she waited for him to change his mind and ask his question.

He rubbed his knuckles against his forehead. "I was just

wondering," he muttered eventually. "This is really embarrassing, but I keep thinking that the reason Mirren won't tell her family about us is because she doesn't see it as a long-term thing." He winced as he looked at Lily. "Did she say anything to you?"

She felt a jolt of sympathy for him. "She didn't say much." Frowning, she tried to recall her conversation with Mirren. "I definitely got the impression she likes you a lot – and she said she was planning on telling her sons soon."

"Okay. That's good. Sorry, this is awkward, isn't it?"

She shook her head. "It's fine."

"Are you okay?" he asked, narrowing his eyes. "You look a little peaky."

She inhaled through her nose, trying not to focus on the slight discomfort in her stomach. It was probably down to stress.

Or so she hoped.

"I think I'm okay," she said, before hopping out of the car and heading for the comfort of home.

Chapter Twenty-Eight

WHEN LILY TOOK herself to bed that evening, it was with a sense of impending doom. Maybe Flynn had been right that she should have thrown away the ice cream and delayed opening the shop. Ingesting something you suspected of containing poison seemed less sensible as the day went on.

The message from Flynn asking if she wanted him to come and sleep on her couch did nothing to calm her nerves. His implication that she may need medical assistance wasn't subtle. She told him she was fine, then messaged again when she was tucked up in bed and asked him to keep his phone on loud.

It took her a few minutes when she woke to figure out her confusion. She had that gnawing feeling that something wasn't quite right, which was quickly replaced by relief when she realised it was merely surprise at having slept the whole night without waking to stomach pains or any other signs of poisoning.

Apparently, the mint choc chip ice cream was okay.

Sitting up in bed, she replied to Flynn's early morning message to inform him she'd survived the night and had no ill effects from the ice cream. She'd need to test the other flavours, but it was the mint leaves which had been her main concern.

With thoughts of opening the shop in two days fresh in her mind, she hopped out of bed, intent on making more batches of ice cream. She'd stick to recipes which didn't require her to use supplies from the garden centre, just to keep her nerves at bay. She could make plenty of double chocolate chip, and another batch of vanilla.

While she worked, she kept an eye on the door, wondering if Flynn would materialise.

The bell above the shop door made a slightly different sound if someone opened it in a hurry. Lily hadn't even realised she was so accustomed to the specifics of the jingling sound, but her head shot up and she knew before she saw the stricken look on Flynn's face that something wasn't quite right.

"You need to help me," he hissed as he shot across the shop floor and slid into the back room to disappear around the corner.

"What's going on?" She stepped back there. "Where's my coffee?"

"I'll get you a coffee if you hide me."

"If I do *what?*"

"You heard." He slumped against the wall, breathing heavily.

"Hide you from who?" She'd only just got the words out when the bell jingled again, back to its sedate tinkle.

"From *her*," Flynn mouthed, pointing towards the door.

Lily looked through the shop at a tall blond woman stepping inside. "You have got to be kidding me?" she muttered under her breath. Her eyes slid to Flynn, who pressed his palms together in a prayer like gesture.

"Please," he mouthed, his eyes widening to a pathetic puppy dog expression.

"Hi," the blonde said, drawing Lily's attention. "Sorry to bother you."

"I'm not open yet," Lily said, stepping into the doorway but keeping Flynn in her peripheral vision.

"I know." She pushed her long glossy locks behind her shoulders. "I was just looking for Flynn."

Lily tugged on her earlobe while attempting a puzzled expression. "Who?"

"Flynn." She rested a hand on her hip. "The tall, dark-haired guy who just ran in here."

"You mean PC Grainger?" Lily glanced behind her as though looking for him and caught the pathetic look on his face as she did. "Yep. He just ran through here. Went straight out the back door. I think he was chasing a criminal."

Her stomach clenched with annoyance – at herself for covering for him, and at Flynn for being a horrible womaniser who ran away from his problems instead of stopping to face the consequences.

"Sure he did," the blonde said, a hint of a smile piquing Lily's interest. She certainly didn't seem like someone who'd been taken in by Flynn's charms and left heartbroken.

"Sorry for whatever he did," Lily said, suddenly furious with Flynn. "He's kind of awful."

The woman waved a dismissive hand in front of her face, then reached into her handbag. "Can you do me a favour and give him this?" She held out a watch. "He left it at my place. I thought it looked expensive."

Lily knew nothing about watches, but the weight of it surprised her. "I think I'd have kept it if I were you," she remarked. "Or sold it."

"I considered it, but I was concerned it might be sentimental, and these things tend to play on my mind."

"Nice of you to get it back to him," Lily said.

The woman cocked her head. "Friends with him, are you?"

"Yeah." Lily automatically glanced behind her. "But I don't always like him very much," she added, loud enough for him to hear.

"Can I give you some advice?" Her eyes flicked over Lily's shoulder and when she spoke again, it was with significantly more volume. "Don't sleep with him. The guy's all charm and not a lot of substance, if you know what I mean?" She winked at Lily and turned on her heel, striding out with her head held high.

After staring after her in awe, Lily stifled a laugh and walked back to find Flynn sitting with his back against the wall.

"That was weirdly fun," Lily said, dangling his watch over him. "I think you met your match with her."

He rolled his eyes. "She knew I was here. She only said that because she knew I was here."

"Or maybe she just thought you were rubbish in bed." Lily grinned and offered him the watch. "Does it have sentimental value?" she asked when he took it.

He frowned at the watch face. "I suppose it might have, for the guy who owns it."

Lily's eyes widened and laughter burst out of her. She slapped a hand to her chest. "It's not yours? Oh, wow! That's brilliant."

"It's not that funny," he said sulkily.

"It's hilarious," she shrieked. "She's the female version of you!"

He stretched his leg out to kick her, but she only kicked

him back and kept giggling. When she calmed down, she offered her hand and pulled him up, then sent him off to get coffee from the cafe.

She should probably have been put out by the weird encounter with one of Flynn's conquests, but it had the surprising effect of breaking the tension between them.

When he returned, they sat at the table nearest the counter. The first hit of caffeine was exquisite.

"Do you ever think about not sleeping around?" Lily asked.

He didn't seem particularly surprised by the question. "I'm not hurting anyone," he said, pushing his chair back from the table and stretching his legs out.

"Maybe not, but doesn't it feel a bit meaningless?"

"Yes." One corner of his mouth twitched upwards. "That's kind of the point."

"Fair enough," she said, not quite disguising the hint of irritation in her voice.

"What other options do I have?" he asked defensively.

"What do you mean?"

"It's not like there's much point in me dating anyone here."

She wrinkled her nose. "Are you commitment-phobic or something?"

"No." He tilted his head and stretched his neck. "I meant while I'm living *here,* there's no point in dating. I'm leaving in a few months. It would be unfair to get involved with someone and then leave them broken-hearted."

"That sounds a little presumptuous," she said, while her insides tightened at the thought of him leaving. Given her nomadic upbringing she really should be used to friendships which didn't last long.

"What do you think about friends with benefits?" he asked, pulling her from her thoughts.

"Excuse me?" Her voice was shrill and full of irritation. It wasn't even the idea of it that was offensive, especially when she thought about their kiss on the beach. They certainly had chemistry. There was just something about the way he'd casually thrown the idea out there that made her want to kick him out of the shop.

"Not *us*." His eyes bulged as he sat up straighter. "That came out wrong... I wasn't suggesting..." His cheeks flushed and he pressed a hand to his forehead. "I meant in general. I wondered about your thoughts on it..." He was blabbering and it was actually quite cute that he looked so mortified. Or maybe she should be offended that he hadn't been suggesting a tweak to their friendship. "I was thinking that if I want to have sex, I basically have three options: one-night stands or a girlfriend or friends with benefits."

"And you've ruled the first two out," she mused.

"No. I only ruled out having a girlfriend. It's you and everyone else around here who isn't impressed with the one-night stand situation."

"You didn't seem too thrilled with it yourself when you were getting chased earlier."

"That's true." He blew out a breath. "I will admit it gets boring. I also haven't done it for a while now," he added sheepishly.

It was irritatingly good to hear that Seren was right on that matter. Irritating, because Lily would really prefer it if she didn't care either way about his sex life.

"You could also just not have sex for a few months," she suggested, pulling her focus back to the conversation.

"I suppose." His eyes sparkled. "I'll be honest, it's not an overly thrilling prospect."

"The problem with friends with benefits is that you need a friend who's happy to sleep with you."

He ran his tongue along his bottom lip and caught her gaze. The silence was excruciating.

"Can I be honest?" Lily said, shifting in her seat. "I'm not entirely comfortable with this conversation."

His face cracked into a smile. "Let's change the subject."

They descended into silence again.

Finally, Flynn leaned onto the table, looking at her with a face full of mischief. "Have you ever done the friends with benefits thing?"

She laughed loudly. "I thought we were changing the subject!"

"Nothing else came to mind. And I'm curious."

"I haven't," she said, shaking her head.

He pursed his lips, looking thoughtful. "You only sleep with people you're in a relationship with?"

"Yes." She cursed the way her cheeks heated.

He must have noticed, because he held his hands up in a defensive gesture. "I'm not hitting on you. I'm being a curious friend, that's all." Silence lingered for a moment before he spoke again. "Should we talk about what happened the other day?"

"Which day?" Lily asked, feigning ignorance.

"The day on the sand dunes," he said, arching an eyebrow. "When you begged me to kiss you and then things got weird between us."

"I did not beg you!" She glared at him. "I barely suggested it and you jumped me."

His eyes sparkled, and she was secretly happy that they were joking about it. "I don't like it when things are awkward between us," he said in earnest.

"Me neither."

"Can we agree that you shouldn't beg me to kiss you again?"

She fought a grin. "Only if you agree not to stick your tongue down my throat because I mutter the word kiss."

"*Mutter the word!*" He cracked up laughing. "You're delusional. You do realise that?"

She beamed at him and drained her coffee before she stood. "I have to eat ice cream."

"Sounds good to me."

"I wasn't offering you any. I'm checking another batch to see if it makes me ill."

"That's really disturbing, you know?"

"Yes. I know. It disturbs me the most. But this is the dark side of owning an ice cream shop that no one thought to warn me about." She wandered into the back room to fetch a container from the freezer.

"What else have you got planned for the day?" Flynn asked when she walked back in.

"After this exciting task, I'm going to pay Gordon Pengelly a visit. Hopefully, he's at the garden centre today." She plucked a bowl from the cabinet and set it aside while she waited for the ice cream to become pliable enough to scoop. "And before you ask, you can't come with me. I get better results when I talk to people alone."

"I'm working in half an hour, anyway." He stood. "I'll talk to you later."

Chapter Twenty-Nine

ARRIVING AT THE GARDEN CENTRE, Lily felt a deep sense of trepidation and hoped she'd be able to catch Gordon alone. His radio interview continued to play on her mind, and she'd like to discover if it was also him who'd spoken to the press on the mainland. If so, she'd be quizzing him on his motives for that.

Surely he could see that the adage of no publicity being bad publicity wasn't always true. Spreading the word that the islands weren't safe for newcomers wasn't the right approach, even if it was true. What they should work on was making sure that the islands were safe.

"Good morning, Lily!" Arthur called out to her as she passed the roses.

"Hi." She couldn't help but smile, given the openness of his features. "How are you today?"

"Fine, thank you." He paused in sweeping the aisle between rows of plants and leaned on his broom. "How are you?"

"Very well, thanks." Something she was currently very

grateful for, considering her endeavours to poison-test her ice cream.

"Ready to pick out some plants?"

"Maybe later," she said. "I actually wanted to speak to Gordon. Is he here?"

"Yes." He pointed inside. "He'll either be in the cafe or the office."

"Thanks," Lily said, before continuing to the door. The pungent scent of soil and leaves in the shop was becoming very familiar. When she reached the cafe, it was all quiet – devoid of both customers and staff.

Inhaling deeply, Lily once again hoped that Gordon would be alone in the office, and that she could avoid another showdown with Sally. Given everything else going on, she hadn't given much thought to Sally's threat of stopping supplies for the ice cream shop, but she supposed she ought to raise the subject with Gordon.

The office door was almost completely closed and Lily knocked lightly. When there was no response, she tried again while pushing at the door.

"Hello!" she called, her eyes doing a quick sweep of the empty room.

She was all set to retreat when her gaze went to the floor beside the desk. *What on earth...*

"Gordon!" Panic strangled her voice as she stepped into the room.

A moment passed with her brain trying to comprehend what she was seeing. Gordon was face down on the carpet, a red streak of blood across his forearm and pooling on the floor beside him.

"Oh my god," Lily mumbled as she approached. "Gordon," she said again, then placed a hand on his back and waited to feel the rise and fall of his rib cage. She let out a relieved sigh when she was certain he was breathing.

Her eyes darted over the room and she felt her heart rate soar before she got her brain in gear enough to realise that she needed to stay calm.

"Stop the bleeding and get help," she muttered, then shot across the room to open the door wide. She called out for Arthur, then decided she needed to be louder and shouted again.

"Ambulance," she said aloud, pulling her phone from her pocket. She almost hit 999 before deciding it would be quicker to cut out the middleman.

"Please don't say you're ill," Flynn said, answering almost immediately.

"I have a problem," she said in a rush. "I'm at the garden centre and I need an ambulance. Quickly."

Flynn's tone was serious. "Are you okay?"

"I'm fine. It's Gordon. I found him unconscious and bleeding. Can you get an ambulance and get up here?"

"I'm on it. Are you alone?"

"Arthur's here somewhere." She caught him walking through the cafe and beckoned to him.

"I'll be there soon," Flynn said. "I'm hanging up to call the hospital, okay?"

She ended the call herself as Arthur approached with his usual cheerful air.

"Did you find Gordon?" he asked, apparently failing to notice Lily's panicked air.

"Yes. He's had an accident." She hurried back to stand beside his prone form. "I've called an ambulance, but I'm not sure what's happened." She frowned as she tried to figure it out. Then her eyes went to the blood. "Why is he bleeding? I need something to stop it." It wasn't gushing or anything, but

187

there was a thick streak across his forearm and a circle of dark red on the carpet too.

Lily went to move beside him, but Arthur's voice suddenly filled the silence and made her pause mid-stride.

"Don't move!" he shouted in a commanding tone that Lily wouldn't have thought him capable of. "Stop right there."

"What's the problem?" Lily asked, a sliver of fear wrapping around her spine as she turned to Arthur.

While her heart rate sped up again, she reminded herself that Flynn was on his way.

Arthur's gaze wasn't on her. In fact, he ignored her entirely as he came to stand beside her.

"It can't be," he whispered, shaking his head and leaning towards the bushy plant on the edge of the desk. "That's not possible."

"Arthur!" Lily snapped. "Can you focus on Gordon? We need something to stop the bleeding. Clean towels or something."

"Yes, yes, of course." He straightened up and finally seemed to register Gordon's unconscious state. "I'll find something." He took a step away, then turned back to Lily and wagged a finger. "Do not go near that plant. Stay right where you are."

"We can talk about plants later," she told him in frustration. "For now, let's focus on helping Gordon."

Arthur hurried away and was back a moment later with a stack of clean tea towels.

"Here." He thrust them at her and immediately switched his attention back to the plant.

For a moment, Lily hesitated, confused by Arthur being more interested in a plant than his incapacitated boss. Then she gave a quick shake of her head and got to work helping Gordon.

"Something cut right through his arm," she said, once she'd dabbed at the blood enough to find the long gash.

"The thorns," Arthur said, then pulled his phone out.

"Do you have a phobia of blood or something?" Lily asked, pressing onto the wound and trying to not jump to conclusions about the way Arthur was intent on pretending his boss wasn't unconscious and bleeding all over the carpet.

"No." His head whipped around and he ran his gaze over Gordon. "The cut came from a thorn."

"Excuse me?" Lily said, her voice oddly squeaky.

"They're illegal in this country. I never thought I'd get to see one in person." His attention shifted again, and Lily watched him hold his phone close to the plant and heard the distinct click of a photo being taken.

"What are you doing?" Lily asked. "Aren't you at all concerned about Gordon?" She stared at Arthur's profile and the glimmer of excitement in his eyes as he continued to photograph the plant. "Arthur!" she snapped when he ignored her completely.

Slowly, he looked over at Gordon again. "You called an ambulance, didn't you?"

"Yes."

"He'll be fine. The thorns are razor sharp, so they'll give you a nasty cut, but the poison isn't deadly or anything."

"Poison?" Lily said, pressing harder on the wound. "What are you talking about?"

"The thorns are sharp," he said, pointing. "They deposit poison directly into the bloodstream to incapacitate their predator."

"Predator?" Lily echoed.

"Wrong word in this case, I suppose. It's fascinating, though, that plants can have such an effective defence mechanism. In nature, they're usually warding off birds and small mammals, but they can take a grown man down too."

Lily blinked slowly. "You're saying this plant is the reason Gordon is currently unconscious?"

"Yes!" Arthur beamed. "Amazing, isn't it? You really have to look closely to even see the thorns. They're the exact same green as the leaves so they blend right in."

"I'm not sure amazing is the word I'd choose," Lily mumbled, eyeing the short, bushy plant with its abundance of vibrant green leaves. "What kind of plant is it?"

"Hmm." Arthur squeezed his eyes closed. "I'm sorry, I'm never very good at the Latin names, and it's an especially long one. In my head I can see how it's written, but I'm afraid I'd bungle the pronunciation."

"Does it have a common name?" Lily ventured.

Arthur nodded vigorously. "The Thorned Sleeping Beauty."

Her eyes went to Gordon's face. Aside from being a little squished against the carpet, he did appear to be sleeping soundly.

"It acts like a natural anaesthetic," Arthur went on. "It's been studied to see if it could be used for surgeries, but its effects are unpredictable."

"So he's just sleeping?" Lily asked.

"Not your standard sleep. He's unconscious, but he'll wake up as though he's been in a deep sleep. The time it takes to come round varies depending on a person's body composition, but people usually wake up groggy after an hour or so, then experience extreme fatigue for anything from twenty-four to forty-eight hours."

"How have I never heard of this before?" Lily asked.

"The plants are rare. They grow mostly in Africa and

people tend to give them a wide berth. In recent years there's been some black-market demand for them."

"Wow." Lily wiped her brow with the back of her hand and felt a wave of relief at the sound of sirens in the distance.

"It's beautiful," Arthur said, attention back on the plant. "I wonder how it got here."

"I imagine Gordon is going to want to know the same thing," Lily said, then sighed heavily.

Apparently, he might have ruffled some feathers with his radio interview.

Chapter Thirty

"We're in here!" Lily shouted when Flynn called out to her.

He stepped into the office, flanked by two paramedics and Sergeant Proctor.

"Are you okay?" Flynn asked her while the paramedics made a beeline for Gordon.

"Stop!" Lily and Arthur shouted at the same time.

Arthur raised his hands, presumably to stop them from getting injured, but in a gesture that actually looked as though he was protecting the plant.

"We need to get to the patient," the female paramedic said, irritation rife in her tone.

"You can," Lily said. "You just need to be careful of that plant. It's poisonous."

"I need to move it out of the way," Arthur said, gingerly dragging it across the desk by the plastic pot.

"I can help," Flynn said, stepping forward.

"No!" Arthur snapped. "Stay away."

Flynn looked at Lily, but it was Sergeant Proctor who

spoke. "What's going on? What on earth happened to Gordon? Is he breathing?"

"Yes," the male paramedic said decisively as he peered at Gordon. "He has a strong pulse," he went on. "Do we know what happened?"

The other paramedic knelt beside Lily and took a sterile pad from her backpack before easing the wad of tea towels from Gordon's arm.

"Looks like a clean wound," she told her colleague. "Deep though. It'll need stitches. How did he end up unconscious?" she asked, eyes darting from Lily to Arthur, who'd dragged the plant to a safe distance.

"He cut his arm on that plant," Lily replied. "The poison from the thorn knocked him out like a sedative, apparently."

The paramedics exchanged a look.

"Arthur can explain," Lily said, distracted by her blood-stained hands.

Flynn handed her a clean tea towel and she wiped at the blood as best as she could while Arthur filled them in on the plant. She was only half listening as she scrubbed the towel over her hands. Blood was trapped under her nails and in her pores and she became increasingly irritated with her failed attempts to remove it.

"Why don't we wait outside and let the paramedics work?" Flynn said once Arthur stopped talking.

He took Lily's arm and guided her into the cafe and to the sink behind the counter. Feeling slightly dazed, she just stood with her hands outstretched while Flynn pumped an excessive amount of soap into them. He rubbed her hands together for her, then gently massaged the soap into every part of her hands. After he rinsed the soap away, he repeated the process.

"Sorry," Lily murmured, feeling as though she was coming out of a trance when he dried her hand with paper towels.

"You okay?" he asked, looking at her intently.

"Yes." She sucked in a lungful of air and felt immediately calmer. "I'm fine." She looked at her hands. "Thank you."

Sergeant Proctor and Arthur had followed them out, but lingered by the door to the office. Arthur craned his neck – unable to keep his eyes off the plant.

"Is everything okay?" The shrill voice broke the silence as Sally Pengelly emerged from a back door. "There's an ambulance outside."

Sergeant Proctor stepped forwards telling her not to panic and explaining there'd been an accident. She didn't seem to panic at all. She only looked confused as the sergeant and Arthur filled her in on the situation.

"A plant did this?" she asked, standing beside Arthur in the office doorway while the paramedics lifted Gordon onto a stretcher. "Are you sure he's going to be all right?" She aimed the question at Arthur, looking up at him with wide eyes.

He nodded. "I've never had any real-life experience of the plant before, but if everything I've read is correct, he'll be fine."

Sally let out a sigh and stepped aside for the paramedics. "Can I come with you in the ambulance?" she asked.

"Yes," the female paramedic replied, then looked at Arthur. "The doctor is going to need as much information as you can give her. I imagine she'll be about as clueless about this as we are."

"I can send her all my research," Arthur said.

"We'll follow you shortly," Sergeant Proctor said to the paramedics before they left. Then he turned to Lily, his brow furrowed. "You always seem to be in the thick of anything going on around here."

"I just came to ask him a few questions," she said, her whole body sagging as the adrenaline wore off.

Flynn squeezed her shoulder. "It's good you found him. That was a fair amount of blood."

"Amazing, isn't it?" Arthur said, his voice full of wonder. "Nature really is fantastic. The thorns don't even appear to be anything out of the ordinary. Yet they can slice you right open."

Sergeant Proctor took a few strides towards the plant, which really didn't look in the least bit menacing.

"Where did it come from?" Flynn asked.

"They're native to Africa," Arthur said.

Flynn tilted his head. "But how did it end up here?"

"No idea," Arthur said.

"Was it only you and Gordon working this morning?" the sergeant asked, shifting squarely in front of Arthur to secure his attention.

Arthur nodded. "Just us."

"Who arrived at work first?"

"I did."

"Was the plant already here?"

"I guess it must have been. But I didn't come into the office. I set up the cafe and then watered the plants and swept up outside."

"Who could have put it here?"

Arthur shrugged. "It's illegal to import them to the UK." The corners of his lips lifted to a small smile. "I wrote a blog piece on it about a year ago."

"Of course you did," the sergeant said with a hint of an eye roll.

"I don't suppose I can keep it?" Arthur asked, a flash of excitement in his eyes.

"No." The sergeant chuckled. "If they're not legal, you can't keep it. I'm not quite sure what we'll do with it, though."

"Burning it seems like a good plan," Flynn said, sticking

solidly by Lily's side. "Once we've figured out how it got here, anyway. For now, I guess we need to take it as evidence."

"I'm not so sure," Sergeant Proctor said. "I prefer your plan of burning it. No chance of anyone else getting hurt that way."

"Surely not," Arthur said sadly. "It's such a rarity. I could put it away safely at my house and no one need ever know about it."

The sergeant snorted a laugh. "Not until you write one of your blog posts telling everyone about it."

"I *would* like to write about seeing one in person," Arthur said eagerly.

"You can't keep it," the sergeant told him firmly. "That's not up for discussion." He shook his head. "Any clue as to what exactly is going on here?"

Lily blinked rapidly when she realised he was talking to her. "My guess would be that someone wasn't happy about Gordon's radio interview..." Her mind whirred, but nothing was making much sense. "It's weird though, because you'd think if someone is trying to scare aware newcomers, Gordon's interview would have helped their cause."

"We don't know that whoever left the plant here was targeting Gordon specifically," Flynn said. "Is he the only person who uses the office?"

"No," Arthur said. "Everyone goes in there. All the staff use it."

"The person who left the plant might not have known that," Lily said, her instincts telling her that the plant was intended for Gordon.

Sergeant Proctor rubbed at his forehead. "I need to get down to the hospital. Arthur, you should come with me and speak to the doctor."

"What do you want me to do about the plant?" Flynn asked.

"Call PC Hill and get him to pick you up and help you transport it to the station. Wrap it in bubble wrap or something so no one else gets hurt. I'll figure out what we do with it later." His gaze shifted to Lily. "Thanks for your help."

"Yeah," she murmured dumbly. "No problem."

Flynn waited until they were alone until he spoke again. "Are you sure you're okay?"

"No." She gritted her teeth as she stared at the innocuous-looking plant. "I'm seriously annoyed. I have no clue who did this. I really thought Gordon was behind the poisonings."

She'd thought she was getting closer to figuring everything out, but now she felt as though she was right back to square one.

As she churned everything over in her mind, none of it made any sense.

Chapter Thirty-One

Lily called Flynn for an update on Gordon the following lunchtime. Apparently, he'd left the hospital early in the morning and was recovering well.

"I think I'll pay him a visit," Lily said, pacing her living room as she spoke into the phone.

"Maybe you should just leave things alone for now," Flynn suggested. "You're opening the shop tomorrow afternoon. You should focus on that."

"I can't." She threw her hand out in exasperation. "How can I concentrate on anything when there's a criminal loose on the island? I need to figure out who it is before they strike again."

"We burned the plant but sent the plant pot over to the mainland for forensic testing. There's a chance we can get fingerprints from it."

"Only a slim chance," Lily muttered. "Because they probably used gloves and even if they didn't, their fingerprints need to be in your database in order for us to know who did it."

"Yeah," he said. "But there's still a chance that it will lead to something."

"If not, we're just sitting around waiting for them to strike again." She banged her fist on the back of the couch. "I'm going to visit Gordon. I need to do something."

"We've already spoken to him at length, but he's ranting a lot. The sergeant isn't inclined to act on what he's saying."

Lily stopped her pacing. "So Gordon has a theory?"

Flynn hesitated for a moment. "He's pointing the finger at Arthur."

"Previously, he was adamant it couldn't be anything to do with Arthur."

"I know, but after his experience with the plant, he's changed his tune. He thinks it's all down to Arthur, but he has no proof, and the sergeant still won't hear a bad word said against Arthur."

"I'm definitely going to speak to Gordon," Lily said, already shoving her feet into her trainers by the door. "I'll talk to you later," she said before she ended the call.

After a brisk walk across the island, she was disappointed to find the gate to the garden centre closed and a sign on it announcing it wouldn't be open again until Monday. She should really have expected that. Sally would be taking care of Gordon until he was fully recovered.

She lingered by the gate, glancing around. Gordon's house was next door to the garden centre – he'd pointed it out to her when she'd first met him. She didn't hesitate long before setting off down the drive to the quaint cottage.

Uncertain of the reception she'd receive, she was relieved when Sally answered the door with a smile.

"I was just thinking about you," she said, stepping onto the doorstep and pulling the door behind her before wrapping Lily in a hug. "To start with, I owe you an apology," she said when she released a slightly dazed Lily. "I was rude the last time we spoke. Honestly, I really believed it was nonsense that someone was deliberately poisoning people, and I was upset with you for thinking it could be someone at the garden centre." She heaved in a ragged breath. "Now, I understand you were just trying to keep people safe."

Lily opened her mouth to speak, but Sally continued before she could get a word out. "I'm so grateful to you for helping my dad. Sergeant Proctor explained how you'd given first aid and called for help." She squeezed Lily's hand. "I love Arthur to bits, but he's useless in a crisis."

Lily had to agree with her there. The only thing Arthur had been interested in was the plant. She liked to think that if she hadn't been there, he'd have done more to help Gordon, but she couldn't swear to it.

"How is your dad?" Lily asked.

"Driving me crazy!" Sally's eyes sparkled as she smiled. "He's clearly exhausted, but he's ranting about needing to find the person who put that plant in his office." She rolled her eyes. "All he actually needs to do is rest, but he won't listen to me."

"Is he up to visitors?" Lily asked.

"Yes! Sorry, I should have invited you in. Come on, I'll put the kettle on and you can say hello – give me a bit of respite from listening to him."

"I think I'd be baying for blood too," Lily said, stepping into the long hallway behind Sally.

"Finally!" Gordon's voice drifted from a room to the left. "Someone who might listen to me. It's very good of you to call over, Lily."

"Go in," Sally said as she set off to the kitchen at the end of the hall. "I'll join you in a minute. Do you want tea or coffee?"

Lily hesitated, still not feeling overly trusting. "Just a glass of water, please."

"I hear I owe you a debt of gratitude," Gordon said, when she walked into the small living room to find him sitting in an armchair with his bandaged arm resting in his lap. Given his pale skin and slumped posture, he looked as though he'd be better off in bed.

"It was nothing," Lily said, but felt her stomach roll at the thought of his blood all over her hands. "I'm glad you're okay. I thought you'd need to stay in the hospital for longer."

"He should have done," Sally called from the kitchen. "The stubborn mule went against the doctor's advice."

"There was no need to stay longer," he insisted, though his shaky voice hinted that even speaking was an effort. "I'm more comfortable at home."

"How's your arm?" Lily asked.

"It's just a cut," he said with a dismissive wave of the hand.

"It was a deep cut," Lily said. "You should take it easy."

"It's this tiredness that's the worst of it," he grumbled. "Sally insisted on closing the garden centre for a few days, so I feel absolutely useless."

"You should concentrate on resting," Lily said, lowering herself onto the threadbare couch.

"I'm not sure how that's possible when there's someone terrorising islanders." He sat forward in his chair. "I hate to say it, but I've been very disappointed in Sergeant Proctor. I always thought he was an asset to the community, but he seems to have dropped the ball on this matter."

"How so?" Lily asked.

Sally walked in and set a glass of water on the coffee table in front of Lily.

"Please don't start on this again," she said, taking a seat

beside Lily. "Sergeant Proctor is taking the matter seriously. The only reason he isn't following up with your demands is because your wild allegations are entirely wrong. That's obvious to everyone except you. Once this poison is out of your system and you're back to your usual self, you'll see that you're not thinking straight."

Gordon ignored her and instead fixed his eyes on Lily. "Realistically, there are only a handful of people who can wander into the office unnoticed."

"I wanted to ask about that," Lily said, leaning forwards. "Where was the plant when you arrived?"

"Just sitting on my desk."

"There was no note or anything? It was only the plant?"

He nodded. "I didn't think much of it. Sometimes Arthur brings in plants he's either grown or ordered. He likes to tell me all about them and will leave them in my office if he arrives at work before me."

"And he arrived before you yesterday?"

"Yes. He was out watering plants when I arrived."

"Was anyone else around?"

"No. We weren't open yet and no one else was working."

"What about deliveries? The food for the cafe?"

"They hadn't arrived yet," Gordon said.

"So what happened exactly when you arrived at the garden centre?"

He paused for a moment, looking thoughtful. "I said hello to Arthur, then went into the office. I noticed the plant straightaway, but like I said, I didn't think it overly unusual so I sat down to drink my coffee and check my emails. But the plant was taking up too much space on the desk so I stood up, intending to move it to the floor. My arm snagged on a branch, or so I thought. I remember a sharp pain and I looked down to see blood on my arm." He shrugged. "Next thing I knew I was waking up in hospital feeling as though someone had sucked every ounce of energy from me."

"When I found you," Lily said slowly. "I called Arthur into the office and he seemed genuinely surprised by the plant."

"He would, wouldn't he? It was all an act. He must have put it there. Who else could have done it? And after all the research he does for his blog, it makes some sense that he'd get it into his head to try out some of these poisons."

"Dad!" Sally chastised. "You're being unfair."

He held his hand up to silence her and kept talking. "I realise no one wants to say it, but everyone was concerned about how Arthur would manage after his mum died. We all wondered if he could cope with living alone."

"He's fine," Sally muttered. "He's perfectly competent. Maybe people were concerned about him, but he's surprised everyone."

"I've noticed changes in him recently," Gordon told Lily. "It's hit him hard to think that Sally will move to the mainland permanently. He was always very fond of her, but he's become a little obsessed. I think he's infatuated with her. He was upset that she couldn't find a job and stay on the island."

"No, he wasn't," Sally retorted. "He's happy for me because he knows moving to Bristol is what I want." She smiled at Lily. "He jokes about coming to visit me if I don't come back often enough. Not that he would – he never leaves the islands."

"I'm telling you," Gordon said. "Something's been off with him recently."

Sally glared at him. "And I'm telling you that you're being ridiculous."

"Can you talk to him again?" Gordon said, eyes fixed on Lily. "If he is behind all of this, I'm sure you can figure it out."

"That's actually not a terrible idea," Sally said wearily. "You could talk to him so you can rule him out of your investigation."

"I'm definitely going to keep looking into it." Lily slapped her palms on her thighs and stood up. "I'll leave you to rest," she said, noticing that Gordon had sunk back into his chair and looked wiped out.

He thanked her for visiting and Sally walked her to the door.

"I can't believe what he's saying about Arthur," she whispered on the doorstep. "I don't understand where it's all coming from. He's also talking about firing him. It'd crush Arthur if he lost his job."

"What did he mean about people being unsure if Arthur could cope with living alone?"

Sally's eyes narrowed. "Arthur is autistic," she said plainly. "I guess some people thought that meant he wouldn't manage to live independently." She gave a lopsided smile. "He has his foibles, but don't we all? And I'm not saying it was an easy adjustment for him when his mum passed away, but losing a parent is difficult for anyone."

"His dad isn't around?" Lily asked.

"He died a few years before his mum, so life hasn't been easy for him, but he has his routines and his garden. And he has a community of people who support him. He thrives here, but I hate to think how hard it would be for him to lose his job."

"Don't worry," Lily said. "Once I figure out who's behind all this, Arthur's name will be cleared and your dad will realise he made a mistake. I'm sure he's just worried and panicking. He's been through a traumatic experience. Maybe you should give him a little leeway."

Sally puffed her cheeks out. "I'll see what I can manage."

Chapter Thirty-Two

BEFORE SHE REACHED the end of the driveway, Lily had her phone to her ear. It felt good that things were back to normal between her and Flynn, and that she could call him without overthinking it.

"Everything okay?" he asked, answering quickly.

"Yeah. Do you know Gordon thinks Arthur is infatuated with Sally?"

"Yes. Sally thinks it's nonsense, and Sergeant Proctor agreed with her."

"Did you also know that he's autistic?"

"The sergeant mentioned it."

"You could have told me."

"I thought it was pretty obvious. I'm also not sure what difference it makes. Would you rule him out of your investigation because of it?"

"I guess not." Her words came out as a question.

"No," he said. "You wouldn't."

"Okay. But with Gordon accusing him, I need to clear his name. And fast before he loses his job."

"What's the plan?"

"I'm on my way to Arthur's place. With his knowledge of plants, he could be the key to figuring everything out."

"I'll meet you there."

She opened her mouth to argue, but thought better of it. From what she knew of Arthur Penrose, he wasn't likely to clam up at the sight of a police uniform.

"See you soon," she said and ended the call.

When Flynn arrived at Arthur's house – on foot and just a few minutes after Lily – she'd already knocked on the door and got no answer.

"He's not here," Lily told Flynn as he stepped onto the garden path.

"Are you sure?" He tipped his head to a wheelbarrow at the corner of the garden, which was loaded up with weeds and chunks of soil.

"He didn't answer the door," Lily said, wandering past Flynn to look around the side of the house. "I guess he probably is around here somewhere." She jerked her chin towards the greenhouse door, which stood open.

There was no sign of Arthur when she stepped into the humid air of the glasshouse, but she assumed he wouldn't have left the door open if he was going far.

"I think there are more plants than the last time we were here," she remarked, wandering through the centre of the greenhouse.

Flynn walked past her to the end of the aisle. "Or maybe the plants have just grown."

"You might be right," Lily agreed, frowning as she eyed the tomato plants in front of her.

"This might be something." Flynn's voice got her attention. He was crouched down, sliding a cardboard box out from beneath the bench at the end of the row.

"What is it?" Lily asked, peering over his shoulder as he

drew back the flaps on the box. Her eyes widened at the pouches of what appeared to be dried herbs. "That's the same herbs that were delivered with the welcome boxes."

"Definitely looks like it," Flynn said. "Don't touch any of it." Shifting the box aside, he leaned under the bench. "There are more plants and flowers down here ... that looks like bunches of cut daffodils at the back..." He moved a potted plant to one side, then winced and withdrew his hand, cursing quietly.

"What was that?" Lily asked.

"A thorn, I guess," he said, moving his hand to his mouth. "That bloody hurts."

As he stood, Lily pulled on his arm to move him out of the way. Her heart pounded as she eyed the familiar plant with its camouflaged thorns. She sucked in a breath, forcing her panic down. "That's one of those sleeping beauty things."

"No way," Flynn said, disbelief thick in his words. "It can't be."

"It is," she said, taking his hand to inspect the damage. "Are you okay?"

"Yeah, it's just a scratch."

"You're bleeding." She rooted in her jacket pocket for a tissue. "Flynn, that's bad."

His brow furrowed as he stared at the plant beside his feet.

"Here," she said, pressing a tissue against the base of his thumb.

"Are you sure it's the same plant?"

"Fairly sure." Lily's eyes darted from his palm to the plant. Carefully, she wedged the toe of her shoe against the pot and pushed the plant under the bench and safely out of the way. "Do you feel okay?"

"I feel fine. I don't think it went deep."

"It's bleeding quite a lot." She pressed a second tissue onto the wound. "Are you sure you don't feel ill, or dizzy or anything?"

"I feel completely normal." Flynn's gaze remained fixed on the plant. "I guess Gordon was right about Arthur."

"Yeah," Lily said, though she was currently more concerned about Flynn than anything else.

"He seems like such a nice guy," Flynn said, his brow wrinkling further. "I'll need to call this in."

"I was sure Gordon was wrong about Arthur." Her stomach knotted, and she realised that she'd wanted him to be wrong about Arthur. Everyone who knew him had insisted he'd never hurt a fly, and she really wanted that to be true.

"This is enough evidence for us to arrest him," Flynn said, but his words came out slowly, as though it was an effort to string the sentence together.

He swayed and clutched at the edge of the counter to steady himself.

Lily put a hand on his back. "Flynn?"

"I don't feel... I'm... My head is..." He squeezed his eyes closed, then opened them and gave a jerky shake of his head as though trying to clear his thoughts.

"You need to sit down," Lily said, trying to keep the panic from her voice.

"I'm okay," he said slowly.

"Yeah," Lily said, forcing reassurance to her voice. "Of course you are, but you should sit down in case you get dizzy. Just for a minute, then you can stand up again and we'll get out of here."

"No, I think I'll be okay." His knees buckled as though they were going to give out, and he slumped against the counter to catch himself. Panic glimmered in his eyes as he looked helplessly at Lily.

"Sit down," she snapped. "I can't catch you if you fall, and I'm fairly sure you're about to collapse. Sit down. Right now."

"Bossy," he murmured as he lowered himself to the ground.

Crouching close to him in the cramped space, Lily took his hand to inspect the wound more closely. "If it didn't cut you as badly as Gordon, maybe the effects won't be so bad." Her insides tightened when she peeled the tissues away. While it was a smooth cut, it was also pretty deep.

"You need..." Flynn started, then seemed to lose his train of thought. "You need to..."

A sound from the garden had Lily's ears pricking.

"Hello?" Arthur called questioningly.

Automatically, Lily ducked down despite already being out of view.

"Lily," Flynn said weakly, as he lowered himself to lie flat on his back. With a feeble arm movement, he pressed a button on his walkie-talkie, but his hand fell away and his eyes closed before he could manage any more.

"Good idea," Lily said, then frowned as Arthur called out again, his voice louder now. "Okay," she murmured, peering at the walkie talkie. "I can figure this out. Press this button, right?" Moving her face close to the device, she whispered frantically. "We need help. There's been an accident. We're on the Isles of Scilly at Arthur Penrose's house. PC Grainger has been poisoned. You need to get in touch with Sergeant Proctor and send him here. And an ambulance too. To Arthur Penrose's house. Quick! Also, I'm turning the radio off so you don't speak and give us away. I need to keep us hidden."

She clicked the radio off before she removed her fingers from the button, hoping someone had heard the message.

"Is someone there?" Arthur's voice was close now and Lily's heart rate went crazy. Flynn's arm twitched and she clutched at his hand while pressing her other hand to his cheek, which was worryingly pale.

"Don't you dare die on me," she said, her voice a hushed whisper. His eyes opened the tiniest slit and relief flood through her. His hand squeezed hers.

"You're not going to die," she told him, annoyed at herself for panicking when she needed to stay calm and reassure him. As his eyes closed again, she moved her mouth beside his ear. "It's going to be fine," she whispered. "You'll sleep for a few hours, and then you'll wake up as though nothing happened. I'll take care of everything until then. There's probably an ambulance on the way already, and Sergeant Proctor will be here any moment, I'm sure of it."

At least she hoped so. But what if the message hadn't gone through? She could get Flynn's phone and call Sergeant Proctor. Or she could call the station from her own phone. She was reaching into her pocket when the greenhouse door opened wider, screeching on its tracks.

"What's going on?" Arthur asked, filling the doorway with his large frame.

"Flynn is hurt." Lily stood to put herself between Flynn and Arthur. "I need to get him out of here."

Arthur might be bigger than her, but Lily knew how to handle herself. Her uncle had always made sure of it.

Slowly, Arthur shook his head. "I'm afraid I can't let you go anywhere."

Chapter Thirty-Three

ARTHUR'S LIPS were parted as he stared at Lily. The piercing shriek of the door as he closed it behind him sent a shiver up Lily's spine. She could definitely defend herself against him. If it were a case of incapacitating him for long enough for her to do a runner, she wouldn't be at all worried.

The problem was, it wasn't herself she was worried about. It was Flynn, passed out on the floor, that had her heart racing and her brain searching for the best way out of the situation.

"Why are you in my greenhouse?" Arthur asked, while his hands fumbled in the pockets of his fleece jacket. "And what did you do to PC Grainger?"

Lily squinted, slightly concerned about what he was searching for in his pockets. "You can't have expected to get away with it forever," she said. "You must have known you'd get caught at some point. This needs to stop now." She looked him right in the eyes and he tilted his head as though trying to figure out what to do with her.

She shifted her gaze to Flynn, comforted by the steady rise and fall of his chest. Maybe the effects really might not be as bad as with Gordon. Maybe he'd only be unconscious for a few moments.

If he could wake up about now, it would be helpful.

"Is he okay?" Arthur patted the pockets of his jeans, then scratched his head.

"Yes," Lily said confidently. "He's okay, and we need to make sure it stays that way. If you help him, everything will be better for you. You can apologise for what you've done, and things won't be so bad. We really need to get him medical attention, though." She pressed her lips together, hoping the tactic would work.

"Yes," Arthur said. "He needs an ambulance. What did you do to him?"

"I didn't do anything," she said. "He touched your plant."

"Which plant?"

She pointed, hoping she wasn't being foolish by drawing attention to the potential weapon in the room.

"Another sleeping beauty." Arthur's eyes widened as he took a step towards it. Then his gaze flicked to Flynn. "His hand is bleeding."

"I know," Lily said. "He needs an ambulance."

"Yes." Arthur patted his chest, then unzipped his jacket and reached inside to pull out his mobile. "I'm going to call Sergeant Proctor. He'll come and arrest you, and he'll send the ambulance. PC Grainger will be fine."

Since she didn't seem to be in imminent danger, Lily crouched beside Flynn and took his hand, partly for comfort and partly to keep the wad of tissues pressed against his cut.

While she listened to Arthur on the phone, she closed her eyes, trying to figure out what on earth was going on.

"He already knew," Arthur said when he ended the call. "The ambulance is already on the way." He frowned, looking as confused as Lily. "Why did you poison him and then call the police?"

"I didn't poison him!" Lily said. "You did. It's your plant."

"It's not mine." He peered at the plant. "They're illegal and Sergeant Proctor said I couldn't have one."

"But it's in your greenhouse," Lily said. "Along with all these other poisonous plants, and the dried herbs and teas, which were in the welcome baskets. You've been poisoning people. The evidence is right here."

"They're not mine," he said flatly. "I don't know where they came from, but they weren't here this morning..." He drummed his fingers against his thigh. "I don't think they were here anyway, but I wasn't paying as much attention as usual because Sally came over yesterday evening and told me not to come to work until Monday. Usually I'd work today and tomorrow. Also, before Gordon got injured she'd said that we could visit the ice cream shop together tomorrow. I don't know if we'll still do that..." He trailed off and scratched his head. "I was quite distracted, but I didn't notice them this morning."

Lily's gaze locked with Arthur's as the sound of sirens reached them, faintly at first, then getting louder.

"You really didn't poison anyone?" she asked.

He shook his head and she was certain he was telling the truth. "I know all about the plants," he said. "It interests me. But I wouldn't hurt anyone. I really wouldn't."

Lily turned her attention to Flynn, continuing to clutch his hand.

"He will be okay," Arthur said. "He'll be fine again in a day or two, just like Gordon."

"I know," she whispered while Arthur muttered about going to meet the paramedics.

She knew in her head that Flynn would be okay, but she

also knew she wasn't going to fully relax until she saw him up and about.

Reluctantly, she moved out of the greenhouse when the ambulance arrived, leaving the paramedics to deal with Flynn. Not that there was much they could do, except get him to the hospital and monitor him until he came round. Hopefully that wouldn't take long since Lily wasn't sure her nerves could take it.

"Everyone's going to think it was me," Arthur said, eyeing Lily intently. "Everyone will think I've been poisoning people, but I don't understand how that stuff got into my greenhouse."

"I suspect someone wanted everyone to think it was you," Lily told him. "Someone is worried about being caught, so they wanted to get rid of the evidence and shift the blame to someone else."

"I don't know anyone who would do that," Arthur said. "Everyone I know is so kind."

"I suspect someone isn't," she said softly. "We just need to figure out who."

Her first thought was Gordon, since he was the one who'd pointed her in Arthur's direction. But Gordon had been poisoned too. She also couldn't see how he could have left evidence in Arthur's greenhouse. Surely it couldn't have been there long without Arthur noticing it, but Gordon had been in the hospital.

Arthur stared at her. "We need to figure it out quickly so they don't hurt anyone else. And so I don't get into trouble. I don't want to go to prison."

"You won't," she said. "I'll figure this out." There was no way whoever was responsible for Flynn lying unconscious was going to get away with it.

"Some people say you're a private investigator," Arthur said.

"Not officially," Lily replied. "But I keep getting caught up in things recently."

"Can you be my private investigator and catch whoever is doing this so I don't have to go to prison?"

She gave him a gentle smile. "I'm already on the case."

"Do you need a sidekick like Sherlock Holmes has? I could be Dr Watson."

That drew a proper smile from her, even if it was only a brief one. She looked over at the greenhouse. "I already have a sidekick," she said sadly.

The sound of cars approaching made her breathe easier.

"What the hell has happened now?" Sergeant Proctor boomed as he stepped out of the police Land Rover. "And why was a civilian using PC Grainger's radio?"

"That was me," Lily said sheepishly.

"Told you." PC Hill got out of a second police car and eyed Lily with amusement. "I knew you'd be involved somehow."

"What happened?" the sergeant asked, looking over Lily's head at the greenhouse.

"We found another of the plants that cut Gordon. Flynn cut his hand on it."

Sergeant Proctor shook his head. "I suppose it didn't occur to him not to touch the plant that can knock you unconscious."

"He didn't do it on purpose," Lily snapped. "He was helping me find evidence of the poisonings."

"Funny that because he told me he was out on patrol."

Anger coursed through Lily's veins. "He *was* patrolling," she growled. "And while doing so, he found a bunch of poisonous plants that account for all the poisoning over the last few weeks. There's also a box with dried herbs and teas, like the ones in the welcome baskets." She drew in a breath. "And now he's bleeding and unconscious, so maybe you could be a little more compassionate."

"Did you say it's the same plant that poisoned Gordon?" PC Hill asked, his voice much softer than the sergeant's. Lily nodded in reply. "So it'll just knock him out for a while and then he'll be groggy, but fine, right?"

"Yes," Arthur said. "There won't be any lasting damage."

The sergeant turned to Arthur. "And why exactly do you have poisonous plants in your greenhouse?"

"He didn't do anything," Lily said, narrowing her eyes. "Someone is trying to set him up, so there's no need for you to start swinging your handcuffs and trying to look heroic." She kept her gaze on the greenhouse as the paramedics brought Flynn out on a stretcher. "Sorry," she mumbled when it occurred to her that taking her anger out on the sergeant wouldn't help her figure out who'd done this.

"I'm not the enemy here, Miss Larkin," he said, but the sergeant's eyes were on Flynn and his features softened as he took a step forwards. "Is he going to be okay?" he asked the paramedics.

The taller of the two men had also been at the garden centre, treating Gordon. He shrugged. "His vitals are stable. It looks the same as with the other guy."

"I'll follow you to the hospital once I've dealt with things here," the sergeant said.

"Can I come in the ambulance?" Lily asked.

"No, you can't," the sergeant replied. "You're not going anywhere until you've explained everything properly."

They watched as the paramedics loaded Flynn into the ambulance and set off for the hospital, then the sergeant walked over to the greenhouse. The rest of them followed.

"Whoever has been poisoning people tried to make it look as though it was Arthur," Lily said, remaining at the entrance to the glass house while the sergeant and PC Hill ventured inside. "But it wasn't him. When Arthur arrived, he thought it was me who'd hurt Flynn and he called the police." She squeezed her eyes shut and shook her head. "*You.* He called *you.* Arthur had no idea what was going on. He doesn't know anything about the plants."

"Actually, I know everything about the plants," Arthur said unhelpfully.

Lily almost laughed at his serious expression. "But you didn't know they were in your greenhouse, or how they got there."

"No." He looked at Sergeant Proctor who'd put a glove on to sift through the packages of herbs in the cardboard box. "I didn't know that. And I would never hurt anyone."

The sergeant scanned the greenhouse until he spotted the sleeping beauty plant. He pointed an accusing finger at it. "That thing needs to be destroyed before it does any more damage."

PC Hill lifted an eyebrow. "Shouldn't we hang on to it as evidence?"

"Possibly." Sergeant Proctor straightened up. "Sod it. I don't want to risk anyone else. Burn the plant, but take photos first." He waved his hand in the air. "Take photos of everything. Then bring everything that could be evidence back to the station."

PC Hill nodded. "Will do."

"I'm going to head to the hospital and make sure PC Grainger is all right. Lily, Arthur, you'll need to go to the station with PC Hill and tell him exactly what happened."

"I'm going to the hospital," Lily said, then grimaced under Sergeant Proctor's icy stare. "I'll give you a statement later, when we know Flynn is okay. It doesn't matter if I tell you what happened now or later, does it?"

"I suppose not."

"I can help PC Hill with the plants," Arthur said amiably.

"Thank you." The sergeant walked out of the greenhouse and took a few steps before turning back. "Be careful!" he called, then let out a long sigh and caught Lily's eye. "I assume you're getting a lift with me?"

She nodded eagerly.

Chapter Thirty-Four

Neither of them spoke again until they were halfway to the hospital.

"What made you go snooping around Arthur's place?" Sergeant Proctor finally asked.

"I wasn't intending to snoop." Not this time, anyway. "I wanted to talk to him because Gordon was throwing accusations around and Sally was worried that her dad might fire Arthur. I wanted to help clear his name."

"Instead, you found incriminating evidence." He gripped the wheel harder. "I've always maintained that this couldn't have had anything to do with Arthur but I'm slightly concerned my judgement might have been clouded. Are you sure we haven't left PC Hill with a dangerous criminal?"

"Arthur isn't dangerous," Lily mused. As the fields rushed by outside, her thoughts drifted back to Flynn looking so lifeless. She swallowed hard and forced her mind away from the unproductive train of thought.

"If it wasn't Arthur, then who was it?" she pondered aloud. "Not Denzel..."

"How did you rule him out?"

Lily winced. "I ruled him out based on his alibi for the time the welcome gifts were delivered, and through an abundance of glowing character references. It's not him. Which means if it's someone from the garden centre, it's either Gordon Pengelly, or his daughter, Sally."

The sergeant snickered. "You think Gordon Pengelly poisoned himself?"

"No." Lily tapped on the dashboard. "I'd ruled him out of my investigations because he was poisoned, but now I wonder..."

The sergeant loosened his grip on the steering wheel. "What?"

"What if he *did* poison himself?"

"Why would he do that?"

"So no one would suspect him?"

"It seems drastic, if you ask me."

"Whoever did this will be looking at prison time, won't they?"

"I'd say so."

"When you weigh it against going to prison – and the entire community finding out you've been poisoning people – a night in hospital probably doesn't feel that drastic."

"It still seems like a stretch."

"It could be Sally," Lily suggested.

"I feel a *but* coming..."

Lily tried to come up with some rational explanation for her gut feeling that it wasn't Sally. "My instincts say it's not." That was the best she could come up with.

"So there's nothing to say it wasn't Sally?"

"No, but..." She rarely had to defend her gut feelings since Flynn pretty much treated them as fact. Apparently, Sergeant Proctor needed more than that. "She seems to have a soft spot for Arthur. I find it hard to believe she'd try to pin everything on him."

"Maybe that's exactly what she wants you to think," the sergeant said. "Or maybe you've got your sights set on the wrong people entirely. Perhaps it wasn't someone connected to the garden centre at all." He pulled up in front of the hospital and looked suddenly sombre. "I'll have to call Flynn's dad, I suppose. Just what I need – explaining to my old friend that his son is in hospital." He huffed out a breath. "I'll get an update from the doctor first."

Lily opened her mouth to speak, but the sergeant was already getting out of the car, so she waited until they were heading into the building.

"You know Flynn's dad?" she asked.

He nodded. "Not well. We worked together back when we were both starting out."

"Did you know Flynn when he was a kid?"

"No." He paused and gave her an odd look. "Michael wasn't together with Flynn's mother. I'm not sure I even knew he had a kid back then. He must have already had Flynn though." He looked vaguely confused as he pulled at the door.

"Is that why Flynn ended up on St Mary's?" Lily asked. "Because of his dad's connection to you?"

"Hasn't he told you about this?"

"Only bits. He doesn't talk much about his dad. What's he like?"

"I don't really know him any more. Not personally. Only by reputation." His attention went to the woman on the reception desk. "I believe you have PC Grainger?"

"He's down in room four," she said, pointing. "Just along the hall. You can wait in the hallway and the doctor will fill you in when she's finished examining him."

"He's all right though?" Lily asked.

"As far as I know," she said with a sympathetic smile.

Striding along the hallway, Lily found room four and knocked quietly.

"We're supposed to wait out here," Sergeant Proctor said, pointing at the orange plastic chairs.

"I'm not great at following directions."

"I've noticed that," he said, a warmth to his voice, which sounded almost like amusement.

Slowly, Lily pushed the door open. A nurse was sticking a needle into Flynn's arm while the doctor stood over him with a stethoscope to his chest. In a hospital gown, he looked even worse than he had done before.

Doctor Redwood straightened up and smiled at Lily. "He's been asking for you."

"Is he awake?" Moving closer to the bed, Lily searched his face, but he seemed completely out of it.

"Not really. He was just muttering a bit." She tipped her chin at Sergeant Proctor. "Hi, Graham."

"Hi. How's he doing?"

"Seems to be okay. It's fascinating. Whatever this plant is, the poison acts like anaesthetic. It's incredible."

"Scary, more like," the sergeant said, while Lily perched beside Flynn and slipped her hand into his, being careful of his freshly bandaged cut. She didn't know if he'd be aware of her, but if it was the other way around, she'd want to know there was someone there with her. That *he* was there.

"PC Hill is disposing of the plant as we speak," the sergeant continued.

"Shame." The doctor stared down at Flynn. "It would be interesting to study it."

"What's *that?*" Lily asked, looking at the drip which the nurse was attaching to the line in Flynn's arm.

"Just fluids," the doctor told her. "We'll keep him

hydrated and monitor him. I've patched up the gash on his hand. That's all we can do for now. Hopefully, he'll wake up before too long."

"Thanks," Lily whispered.

Sergeant Proctor approached the bed and put a hand on Flynn's shoulder in a manner that made Lily feel bad for complaining about his lack of compassion. "I need to go and call his dad, let him know what's going on. That's going to be a weird one to explain."

"If any family members want to speak to me, I'm happy to chat with them," Doctor Redwood said.

The sergeant thanked her and offered Lily a thin smile before he left.

The nurse pressed buttons on the machine beside the bed, then addressed the doctor. "Mr Pengelly is also waiting for you to check his wound."

"Oh." The doctor grimaced. "I didn't need to change the dressing today. I only said that this morning to encourage him to stay longer."

"Should I ask him to come back another time?"

"No. I'll talk to him. Can't hurt to check him over again. Keep a close eye on PC Grainger and let me know if there's any change."

"Gordon is here?" Lily asked.

The doctor nodded as she left.

"I can get you a chair," the nurse said, and returned a moment later with one of the orange plastic seats from the corridor. "Not the comfiest, I'm afraid."

"It's fine. Thank you." She didn't sit, but hovered over Flynn and clung to his hand.

"I'll be back in a few minutes," the nurse said. "Press that red button if there are any problems."

"Thanks," Lily murmured, happy to get a moment alone

with Flynn. As soon as the nurse left, she moved and ran her fingers through his hair. "Flynn?" She whispered, but got no response. After trying again, she pulled the chair closer and lowered herself onto it, then sat trailing her fingers over the back of his hand.

"I have a funny feeling about Gordon," she said. "I know it seems unlikely because he got poisoned too, but I just think it's him. Which isn't helpful, I know. You police always want proof." She smiled sadly. "If you'd like to wake up and help me figure this out, I'd appreciate it." She waited, but he didn't stir.

"PC Hill is collecting all the evidence from the greenhouse," she mused quietly. "Maybe there'll be fingerprints or something." She looked over at Flynn and smiled, imagining what he'd say. She could hear his voice in her head telling her that someone trying to pin a crime on someone else probably wouldn't be stupid enough to leave evidence. Then he'd frown and tell her there were a lot of stupid criminals, so they couldn't rule it out entirely.

"I guess it'll take a while for the forensic team to do their thing," she said aloud. "In the meantime, Arthur is going to be under the spotlight. I told him I'd figure it out." The chair squeaked as she leaned back. "You'd know what to do," she said sulkily.

Her gaze was fixed on Flynn's peaceful features, but her mind was somewhere else entirely. Calmly and methodically, she pondered everything she knew about the poisonings.

Eventually, she went back to the day she'd met with Gordon and drank the awful green smoothie. He'd been the one to pour it for her from the jug in the fridge, but as far as she could remember the rest of the staff had been there too. Gordon had introduced her to them.

Since she hadn't heard of anyone else getting ill after

consuming anything at the cafe, it can only have been her drink which was tampered with. Whoever wanted to poison her must have done it right under her nose.

She growled in frustration, certain she was missing something. If she couldn't figure it out, whoever was responsible might just get away with it.

"Wake up and help me out here," she whispered to Flynn, giving his hand a squeeze.

Once, he'd joked that she'd never been able to solve a mystery without him. She had a sinking feeling that he might have been right.

Chapter Thirty-Five

WHEN THE NURSE RETURNED, Lily wandered to the door, looking up and down the corridor. At the end of the hall, Sergeant Proctor was chatting to the receptionist.

A memory came to Lily out of the blue.

It was during her first visit to the island. She'd been on the ferry with Flynn, trying to figure out who'd killed the guy on the cliffs ... what had Flynn said to her?

Sometimes in policing we bluff...

Back then, he'd asked her to give him her best guess as to the perpetrator. Then he'd pretended to know more than he did and watched how the suspects reacted.

Her breath hitched as she looked back at Flynn. Deep in her gut, she was sure she knew who'd done all this. She just needed to trust her instincts the way Flynn always did.

After a couple of deep breaths, she pulled her shoulders back and strode along the hall.

"Sergeant Proctor!" Lily called out, stopping him in his tracks as he walked towards the door. When he turned, she shouted again. "I know who's been poisoning people."

He squinted, presumably annoyed with her for screeching

so loudly in the hospital. The stern look he gave her didn't deter her.

"It's Sally Pengelly," she called out, loud and confident. "You need to arrest her before she hurts anyone else."

The sergeant's eyes flashed with annoyance as she approached him.

"Calm down," he hissed. "Whatever theory you have, we can go somewhere private and you can tell me properly. There are sick people here and you're yelling loudly enough to disturb them all."

"Sorry," she said, barely lowering her voice at all. "It's definitely Sally Pengelly, though. I just figured it all out. It's obvious, if you think about it..." She trailed off as Gordon Pengelly stepped out of a room further along the corridor.

The grimace hit her lips immediately, and she did her best to look sheepish.

"You're right," she said to sergeant Proctor quietly. "This should probably be a private conversation." She took a step closer so that only he could hear. "We need to be quick though, before she figures out we're onto her."

"What's going on?" Gordon asked, striding over to them. "I heard Sally's name mentioned."

Lily offered him a weak smile. "Unfortunately, there's been another casualty. PC Grainger was cut by one of those sleeping beauty plants. He's currently unconscious."

"Oh, dear," Gordon said, his lips twisting to the side. "I'm sorry to hear that. What's that got to do with my daughter?"

"I'm very sorry," Lily said gently. "But there's evidence that Sally is at the root of these crimes."

Heat blazed up Gordon's throat and his cheeks flushed too. "That's absurd. She'd never be involved in anything like that."

Ignoring him, Lily appealed to the sergeant. "We really

need to find her. I'm concerned she's going to do something else. We need to put a stop to this. And quickly." Her gaze went to Gordon. "Is she here with you?"

"No. She dropped me off. I was going to call her to pick me up." He gave a small shake of the head and puffed his chest out as he addressed Sergeant Proctor. "These allegations are ridiculous. I hope you're not going to pay her any attention."

The sergeant looked down at Lily. "You mentioned evidence? You're sure it's Sally?"

She nodded. "I can explain everything in the car, but we should go and find her."

"You can't be serious." Gordon Pengelly huffed out a laugh. "You're letting some clueless girl do your job instead of doing proper police work?"

"I'd hardly call her a girl," the sergeant said gruffly. "And I've never been above taking information from our residents. That's what gives our community strength. We work together."

"Of course," Gordon said, abashed. "I just don't understand how she can point the finger at Sally."

"Sally did it." Lily looked pleadingly at Sergeant Proctor. "I know we don't always see eye to eye, but please trust me on this. We need to find her. Right now."

"You can't go harassing people based on hearsay," Gordon said. "Surely you're above that, if nothing else."

"I don't intend to harass anyone," Sergeant Proctor said flatly. "If Sally is innocent, like you say, then she's got nothing to worry about." He tipped his head towards the door and Lily fell into step beside him.

"She'll be looking at jail time, won't she?" Lily asked as they made for the door. The sergeant gave her a puzzled sidelong glance, but she barely registered it. "Even if she didn't physically touch Flynn, this will still count as assaulting a police officer, won't it?" She didn't wait for an answer. She didn't need one. "I hope she gets locked up for a very long time."

Outside the building, Lily finally stopped wittering.

"You're sure it's Sally?" the sergeant asked, stopping in front of the Land Rover.

"No," Lily whispered. "I'm not sure of anything."

His eyeballs looked as though they might take flight from their sockets. "Then what the hell was all that about?"

"Shh! Just trust me. I have a hunch." She glanced back at the hospital doors. "Let's just wait a minute…"

"I have no idea what is going on," Sergeant Proctor grumbled.

Lily was worrying that she'd got everything wrong when Gordon stepped out of the hospital.

"Wait!" he shouted. "Just wait. I need you to explain this. I can't for the life of me understand why you'd think Sally was behind any of this."

"I'm afraid we'll have to fill you in later," Lily said, heading to the passenger door of the police car. "We're in a rush."

"It wasn't Sally," Gordon said firmly. "Why is no one looking into Arthur like I told you to?"

"I did look into it," Lily said. "And what I found led me to Sally." She opened the car door. "Get in the car," she muttered to Sergeant Proctor.

"I'm sorry," the sergeant said to Gordon. "I will keep you updated, but I have to follow all lines of enquiry."

"I don't see what the rush is?" Gordon said, putting a hand on the passenger door to stop Lily from closing it.

She eyed him warily. "People keep being poisoned. You don't think that warrants some urgency?"

"I mean, what's so urgent that you can't take a few minutes to explain your logic? Not that I believe there is any logic to your allegations."

"Fine." Lily turned in the seat. "For a start, I'm fairly sure it was Sally who tried to poison me."

"What are you talking about?" Gordon asked.

"I got ill after drinking a smoothie from the garden centre. That's how I always knew it was someone who worked at the garden centre. Sally had transferred my drink into a takeaway cup and I'm sure that's when she added something to it." To avoid having to elaborate, she didn't pause. "For a while I thought it was Arthur, and then Denzel, but finally I narrowed it down to you or Sally. Obviously, it can't have been you or you wouldn't have fallen victim to the sleeping beauty. Also, since you were in hospital, it can only have been Sally who planted evidence at Arthur's house." Finally, she stopped for breath.

"What do you mean, she planted evidence?"

"Someone left evidence of the poisonings at Arthur's place to incriminate him."

"How can you know that? Surely if you found poisonous plants, that's evidence that Arthur was the one behind all this, which is what I kept trying to tell you."

"It wasn't Arthur," Sergeant Proctor said in a tone that brooked no argument. He hadn't got into the car, but had moved beside Gordon. "We know someone tried to set Arthur up. We're currently trying to figure out who. The forensic team will go over the evidence from Arthur's house. With any luck there'll be fingerprints."

"This is ridiculous," Gordon said, looking hot under the collar. "You can't honestly think that Sally sneaked into Arthur's greenhouse and left a bunch of poisonous plants. She and Arthur are very close friends. She wouldn't do that to him."

Lily fought a smile. Backing Gordon into a corner felt immensely satisfying. "Who said anything about a greenhouse?"

"What?"

"You said the plants were in Arthur's greenhouse, but I never said that."

Once again, the skin of his neck turned red. "I just assumed. It seems like the logical place."

"The logical place to plant evidence?"

"That's not what I..." He opened and closed his mouth repeatedly, then turned and looked at Sergeant Proctor. "Are you really going to let her speak to me like this?"

"I think she has a point. It is odd that you knew the plants were in the greenhouse. Given the gravity of the crimes, I'm afraid I'm going to have to take both you and Sally into custody until we've sorted this out. For the safety of the island residents."

"Not Sally!" he shouted. "Sally had nothing to do with any of this. Keep her out of it."

"How do you know she had nothing to do with it?" the sergeant asked pointedly.

He closed his eyes for a moment. "It was me." He threw his hands out. "It was me and nothing to do with Sally. She didn't know what was going on."

Lily wanted to say something but decided to leave space for Gordon to seal his own fate. "It wasn't even so bad," he said, looking desperately at the sergeant. "A few people got ill, that's all. There was no real harm done."

"Considering Glynis Ward is still in hospital on the mainland and one of my officers is currently unconscious, I'm going to disagree with you there." Sergeant Proctor's features were set in a hard frown. "Why on earth would you do this?" he growled.

"Because the island is being overrun! Anybody who wants to waltzes over here to set up home and open their businesses. And while they're at it, they drive the true Scillonians away. You must see how difficult it is for local kids to get jobs here. How many youths move to the mainland to get work each year?"

"They move because they want a different life," the sergeant said. "Most of them move by choice, not because they can't find jobs."

"What about Sally?" Gordon snapped.

"She didn't want a job here," Lily said. "But even if she couldn't find a job, it doesn't give you the right to poison people."

"What were you thinking?" the sergeant asked.

"Arthur had laid everything out in his blog," Gordon said as though Arthur were still to blame. "I only wanted to give it a go. It's not as though I was trying to kill anyone."

"Where did you get your hands on that sleeping beauty thing?" the sergeant asked.

"I got a couple of them imported ages ago. It's actually not difficult."

"Why?" Lily asked.

"Arthur had been going on about them and I was intrigued."

Words failed Lily.

"And you put evidence in Arthur's greenhouse," Sergeant Proctor said. "You tried to set him up."

"That lad is too stupid to defend himself properly. Everyone would have believed it was him."

The sergeant glared at him. "You'd have let him take the blame?"

"I wouldn't have needed to blame anyone if she hadn't been asking so many questions." He jabbed a finger in Lily's direction. "I was only going to make a few people ill and then cause a bit of a stir... make it seem like the islands aren't such a friendly place... but she just kept asking questions and messing everything up."

Lily blinked rapidly as she tried to comprehend what she was hearing.

"I'm going to need you to come down to the station," Sergeant Proctor said, suddenly business-like.

"You weren't serious about prison, were you?" Gordon asked.

"Very. Food tampering and poisoning are serious offences. You could also be charged with grievous bodily harm."

Gordon shook his head. "I need to go and explain everything to Sally."

"I'm afraid the only place you're going is to the station with me. You can call Sally later."

"No. I'll come to the station later, but I really need to explain this to Sally in person."

"I don't think you understand," Sergeant Proctor said. "I'm arresting you."

Gordon's eyes bulged. "I thought you'd just need to question me to start with. And surely I need a lawyer."

"You'll definitely need a lawyer," the sergeant said. "But we'll get to that later..."

Lily hopped out of the car. "Before you read him his rights and all that fun stuff, I think I'll say goodbye."

"I'll need to speak to you later too," the sergeant said to Lily, while he opened the back door for a dumbfounded Gordon.

Lily pointed at the hospital. "I'll be with Flynn."

Chapter Thirty-Six

THE RUSH OF ADRENALINE SUBSIDED, turning Lily's insides jittery as she walked back to Flynn's room. He stirred when she walked in and she darted to the bedside, but he only groaned before his facial muscles slackened and he slipped back into sleep.

She pulled up the chair and kept hold of his hand while she waited for him to properly wake up.

The nurse came to check on him a couple of times over the next hour or so. When the door opened a third time, Lily looked up to find Sergeant Proctor creeping in.

"Hi," he whispered. "Has he woken up yet?"

"Not properly." She tilted her head and caught the sympathetic look the sergeant gave her.

"Here's what I can't figure out," he said quietly. "Did you really suspect Sally had been poisoning people?"

She gave a small shake of her head. "No. I was fairly sure it was Gordon. I knew he was in the hospital and I thought the easiest way to get him to admit to everything would be to accuse Sally."

"Clever." He rested a hand on the edge of the bed, beside Flynn's leg. "Unconventional, but clever."

"I'm just happy we can put a stop to all of this. He won't get away with it, will he?"

"No. I've spoken to colleagues on the mainland who agree that he's a danger to the community. PC Hill will take him over on the ferry tomorrow and he'll be held on remand until he goes to court for sentencing. He's looking at a prison sentence."

"Good," Lily said, then looked at him questioningly. "When did Gordon have time to put the stuff in Arthur's greenhouse?"

"Right before he poisoned himself with that plant. He knew the investigation would heat up and decided he'd point us in Arthur's direction."

"It didn't make sense," Lily said. "When I found him in his office, it was as though the plant had cut him and he'd collapsed immediately. With Flynn, it wasn't instant. There was time for him to deal with the cut before he passed out. Gordon would have been able to try and stop the bleeding or call for help. The back of his arm was also an odd place for it to have cut him if it was an accident."

"That's what made you think it was him?"

"It didn't add up." She let her head sink to her arms, resting on the bed.

"You look exhausted," the sergeant said. "You should go home. PC Grainger is in good hands here."

"I'll just hang around a little longer. I want to be here when he wakes up."

The sergeant nodded. "I need you to make a statement, filling in the blanks about all of this."

"I will," she said wearily. "It doesn't need to be today though, does it?"

"No. Not today." The sergeant straightened up. "I left a message for Flynn's dad but I haven't heard from him. I might go and try him again."

"Okay." Lily couldn't even be bothered to lift her head.

"Go home," the sergeant said. "You need to rest. Aren't you opening your shop tomorrow?"

"Maybe." She couldn't think about that. She wasn't sure she'd be able to face it, and would likely postpone. "I'll go home soon," she whispered, then said goodbye as the sergeant left.

She'd just closed her eyes when she felt Flynn's fingers curl around hers. In an instant she was alert again and searching his peaceful features.

"Lily," he murmured without opening his eyes.

"I'm here." She put a hand on his chest.

"Arthur," he mumbled, lips barely moving.

"It's fine. Everything is fine."

"You're okay?"

"Yes. You're in the hospital, but you're going to be all right. I'll explain everything when you're feeling better."

"Good." His features relaxed as he slipped back into sleep.

Lily pressed the call button and updated the nurse when she arrived. The doctor came to check on him too and he woke again, just enough to mutter that he felt okay, but was tired.

Doctor Redwood insisted that he'd likely sleep all night and kindly told Lily to go home.

"I'll just stay a little longer."

She'd stay for another half an hour, she told herself, attempting to get comfy on the orange chair. After that, she'd go home and get some sleep.

Flynn felt as though he was under water, fighting to reach the surface. Some invisible pressure was pushing him down and his thoughts were trapped in a thick fog. Finally, his eyelids obeyed him and he blinked at the stark room.

Where the heck was he?

His hand throbbed and the dull pain seemed to clear his thoughts.

He'd cut it in Arthur's greenhouse and the poison had made him light-headed. The dizziness hadn't bothered him as much as the thought that he'd been about to pass out and leave Lily to deal with a deranged lunatic who'd been poisoning people.

Lily had been in danger and he'd been helpless to do anything. Presumably she'd figured it out, since he was reasonably certain he was in hospital. His instincts told him she was fine.

Again, the throbbing in his hand drew his attention. He lifted it to find it wrapped in a bright white bandage. Pressure against his thigh told him he must have done something to his leg too, though he had no recollection of that.

"Oh," he muttered, as he looked down at what had felt like a boulder wedged against his leg. If it hadn't required so much effort, he'd have smiled at the sight of Lily, fast asleep in a chair with her arms and head slumped onto the side of the bed and using his leg as a pillow.

She couldn't possibly be comfy, but he couldn't bring himself to wake her. Ignoring the soreness in his palm, he lay his bandaged hand softly over the back of her head and closed his eyes again as he tangled his fingers in her hair.

He slipped in and out of sleep, comforted by Lily's presence. Only when the pins and needles spread to his toes, did he give her a gentle nudge.

"I might lose a leg if you don't stop cutting off my circulation soon," he said, his voice hoarse.

She wiped at the side of her mouth as she woke.

"Sorry," she mumbled, sitting up.

He wriggled his toes and moved his foot from side to side.

Her hair was stuck to one side of her face and creases marked her cheek. She stood and arched her back while gently moving her head from side to side.

"It wasn't comfy for me either," she said through a yawn. Her eyes widened as though only just registering where they were. "How are you?" she asked, peering at him. "You look better. Do you feel better?"

"I feel terrible," he said groggily. "Like I have the mother of all hangovers."

Lily slumped back into the chair. "You scared me," she said softly.

He reached for her and when she took his hand it felt like the most natural thing in the world. He had no memory of what had happened since he passed out in that greenhouse, but he'd swear that Lily had been there the entire time, holding his hand.

"I really didn't think it was Arthur," he said and felt a pang of sadness that he'd been wrong about him.

"It wasn't," Lily said.

"What?" A wave of exhaustion hit him and it was a battle to keep his eyelids open.

"Are you okay?" Lily asked. "Sleep if you need to. I can fill you in later."

"Carry on," he said, but closed his eyes. "I want to hear about it." He brushed his thumb softly across Lily's palm. "Unless you want to go home and sleep?"

"I can tell you before I go," she said.

He nodded. "You may need to tell me again when I'm more alert. And if I fall asleep while you're telling me, don't take it personally. It's not a reflection of your storytelling."

"I won't take it personally," she agreed. "And I'm probably going to tell this story so many times in the next weeks that you'll get sick of hearing it."

He smiled and sank back into his pillows. "What happened after I passed out? I remember hearing Arthur in the garden and you using my radio. After that it's a blank."

"I was totally freaking out," she told him, then launched into a full account of everything he'd missed.

Since he couldn't keep his eyes open, or contribute to the conversation, he continued moving his thumb against her hand so she at least knew he was listening.

He struggled to keep up with the chain of events, but it wasn't only the overwhelming tiredness that made it difficult to concentrate on the words. The softness of her skin under his thumb took most of his attention.

"I should probably go and let you rest," she said eventually. Her voice was so quiet that it was clear she didn't know if he was still awake.

He was fairly sure he'd nodded off again, but woke up at the mention of her leaving. Forcing his eyes open, he held her gaze. "It's the opening of the shop today, isn't it?" He thought that was right, unless he'd slept for longer than he thought.

She groaned. "I'm going to postpone it."

"No." He shuffled to get more upright and hopefully force some alertness to his brain. "You have to do it. You've already put it off for long enough."

"I don't think another week will make any difference."

"What time is it?"

"Seven a.m."

Flynn looked around. "Where are my clothes and all my stuff?"

"In the cupboard, I think." She untangled her fingers from his and walked over there. "Your uniform is in here."

He asked her to find his phone from the pocket.

"Sergeant Proctor called your dad yesterday to let him know you were in the hospital."

"Great," Flynn said unenthusiastically. To be fair, he supposed it would seem like the appropriate thing to do. How was the sergeant to know that his dad was about the last person he'd want informed in an emergency?

"Everything all right?" Lily asked after passing him his phone.

"Yeah." He tapped on the phone and searched his calls and messages. Finally, he admitted to himself that his dad hadn't been in touch. He was lying in a hospital bed and he didn't even care enough to send a message.

He set his phone down on the bed and focused on Lily. "What time is the opening for the shop?"

"It's supposed to be two o'clock but I really don't think it's going to happen today."

"Why not?"

"Because I've barely slept. That's one reason. I'm also not prepared."

"Yes, you are. The ice cream is ready to go. What more do you need?"

"A bit of energy and some positivity would probably be a good thing," she said wearily.

"Go home and sleep for a few hours. You'll be fine."

She shook her head. "I'm not in the mood for any kind of celebration. It wouldn't feel right..."

"Because of Gordon? It can be a double celebration. You figured out another mystery. That's something to celebrate."

"I meant it wouldn't feel right without you there. When I thought about opening the shop, I imagined you there. Just for moral support or whatever, but I don't want to throw a party when you're in hospital."

"I'll be there," he said confused. "I'll sleep for a little longer, then I'll be fine."

"The doctor said you'll need to stay for forty-eight hours at least."

"No way. That's not happening."

She shifted closer to the bed. "No offence, but you look terrible."

"I'm tired, that's all. Nothing a few hours' kip won't fix." He ignored the heaviness which had settled through his entire body and made him feel as though he were pinned to the bed. "The hospital gown makes me look worse than I am. It's not my style." He tilted his head. "Could you do me a favour and nip back to my place and grab me some clothes before you go home?"

"I can do that," she said. "But you can't leave here until tomorrow."

"I'm not missing the opening of the shop."

"In that case, I'm definitely not opening today. I'll postpone until next weekend."

"I want you to do it," he said. "And I definitely don't want to be the reason you put it off."

She took a breath, drawing all the patience she could muster. "Fine. I'll open the shop today. But you have to promise you'll stay here and rest."

He hesitated before he reluctantly agreed. "Ted will help you. And Seren and Kit too. And the rest of the Trenearys, no doubt."

Lily sucked in a dramatic breath.

"What's wrong?"

"Nothing." She pulled her phone from her pocket and winced at the screen. "Yep, I have a load of messages and missed calls from Seren. And a couple of messages from Kit and Ted." Her shoulders slumped. "Dante has been trying to call me too. He'll be after an update. I don't think I can deal with him."

"Just ignore him for now. You have other stuff to deal with. And apparently lots of support." He pointed at the phone.

She tapped on the screen. "Seren will have been worried when I didn't reply. I'll just message and let her know I'm fine and will call her in a bit."

"And tell her you need her help with the shop later," Flynn added, though she didn't seem to register him. "I'll bet she already knows everything that happened anyway. You know what it's like here... news spreads fast."

"True." She pocketed her phone and stepped closer to him.

"You are going to open the shop today?" he asked.

"Yeah," she said reluctantly. "I just need some sleep and then I'll feel better about the whole thing." She rested a hand on his arm. "You really do look shocking."

He tried to smile, but didn't have the energy. "I'm okay," he said, then grabbed at her hand when she went to move away. "Sorry," he said weakly.

"What for?"

"Passing out on you and leaving you to deal with everything." He felt slightly sick when he thought back to the moment he realised he was going to pass out and leave her vulnerable.

"It's not as though you did it on purpose." Again, she went to move away and he tightened his grip to stop her.

"Thanks for staying with me," he said, eyes locked with hers.

Her throat bobbed as she swallowed. "You'd do the same for me. Now let me find your keys. Apparently, I'm off to root around in your underwear drawer."

"You know I'd return *that* favour anytime," he said cheekily.

She gave his leg a gentle shove. "Shut up and go to sleep."

He was fairly sure he didn't have much choice in that. He'd never felt exhaustion like it, but he managed to keep his eyes open to watch Lily rummage through his pockets for his keys.

"When I come back, I'll leave your stuff at the front desk so I don't disturb you," she told him when she found them.

"Okay."

"Sleep well."

"Lily?" he muttered when she was almost at the door. "If you're not too knackered after the opening, you could come back and tell me how it went." When she didn't respond immediately, he felt like the most demanding person in the world. She hadn't left his bedside all night and now he was asking her to come back again at the end of her busy day. "Or tomorrow," he added quickly. "I'll talk to you tomorrow. You'll be too tired to come back later."

"I'll come back," she said, quiet but firm. "See you tonight."

Chapter Thirty Seven

ONCE SHE'D DROPPED Flynn's things off at the hospital, Lily trudged back to the shop feeling defeated. Maybe it was tiredness clouding her thoughts, but she really didn't think she could open the shop.

With her mind racing, she didn't notice the figure loitering by the shop until she got near.

"I don't know why I'm surprised to see you here," she told Ted. "Flynn called you, I guess?"

"Yes. He said you needed help."

"Thank you," she said, sagging into his hug. "Did he tell you everything that happened?"

"I got the broad strokes." He kept a reassuring hand on her shoulder when he took a step back. "Is he doing okay? He said he was fine, but he has to stay in hospital?"

"Just for another night and mostly as a precaution, I think. He looks rough, but he's all right."

"Glad to hear it. No offence, but you look pretty rough yourself."

"I stayed at the hospital overnight," she told him, slipping the key into the lock. "I didn't sleep too well."

"You've got a few hours to sleep before the shop opening."

"I don't think I'm going to open today," she said, stepping inside.

"Flynn thought you might say that. I'm supposed to convince you otherwise."

"It's not because of Flynn," she said, flopping into the nearest chair. "It's because I now know for a fact that Gordon was sabotaging businesses and I don't know if he's contaminated the ice cream somehow. I've tasted most of the batches with ingredients from the garden centre, but I can't be sure." She ran her hands through her hair. "How can I serve it to children without being certain I'm not poisoning them?"

Ted's grimace wasn't exactly reassuring.

"I can't, can I?" she asked, needing guidance from someone who wasn't sleep deprived and stressed.

"Where's Gordon now?" Ted asked after a thoughtful silence.

"At the police station." She checked her watch. "PC Hill's taking him to the mainland today, but the ferry doesn't leave for a while."

"Okay," Ted said, returning to the door. "I'll head to the station."

"What are you doing?"

"If he tampered with your ice cream, he might admit to it now. It'll be in his best interests to confess before anyone else gets ill."

"That's a good idea." She sighed. "Should I come?"

He shook his head. "I'll figure it out."

Upstairs, she resisted the temptation to get into bed. She needed to wait and see what Ted found out, and then either get to work finishing her preparations for opening the shop, or – more likely – get to work spreading the word that she was postponing.

Sinking into the armchair in the living room, she stared out of the window at the sandy beach and the hypnotic waves washing onto the shore. When her phone rang, she grabbed at it, thinking it would be either Ted or Seren.

An unknown number flashed on the screen. She answered it with a questioning lilt.

"Hi," the familiar voice said. "It's Sally."

"Hi," Lily said, sitting upright. "How are you?"

"Honestly, I don't know how I am, but I wanted to call and apologise."

"What for?"

"For my dad," she said, as though it was obvious. "I can't believe what he's done. This all feels completely surreal, but I'm so sorry. I know he tried to poison you as well as the others."

"You don't need to apologise. It was your dad, not you."

"I know, but I feel as though I should have realised what he was up to. I honestly didn't have a clue. Even now, I can't comprehend that he deliberately set out to hurt people. I would never have thought him capable of it."

"It must be a lot to take in."

"Sergeant Proctor says he'll go to prison." Sally's voice wobbled, and she paused for a moment. "I just can't believe any of this. And he tried to get Arthur in trouble. I'm so angry with him."

Lily nodded, but wasn't sure what to say.

"Ironically, he's probably going to get what he wants now," Sally said tearfully.

"How do you mean?"

"I mean, he's claiming all this started because I couldn't get a job here, and he was upset about me leaving, but with him not here, I guess I'll stick around and take care of the garden centre. At least for the time being.

That's if we even have any customers once everyone finds out what Dad did." She exhaled a shuddering breath. "I should have told him the truth about wanting to leave the island."

"Don't blame yourself," Lily said. "I'm sure there was more going on in his head than just being angry that you couldn't find a job. Poisoning people isn't a normal response to that."

"You're right," Sally said. "I think it was more like a trigger. My mum left him, you know?"

"I didn't know that." Somehow, Lily had always assumed that Sally's mum had passed away, but she'd never really thought too much about it.

"She left when I was thirteen. I had the choice of going with her, and I think I'd have gone if I hadn't felt so sorry for my dad. Mum wanted a career and felt she couldn't achieve what she wanted living here. She's a very successful lawyer now, in Bristol."

"Is she part of the reason you wanted to move there?"

"Yes, but again, I felt bad for my dad. I guess I was right to worry about how he'd handle it." She fell silent again for a moment. "Have you seen PC Grainger? The sergeant said he was recovering, but I feel terrible."

"He's okay," Lily told her, then took a breath. "Do you really think you'll stay on St Mary's now?"

"Arthur says he can look after the garden centre, but I can't leave him to run the place alone. Though I guess I may end up closing it, since it wouldn't surprise me if people boycott the place. I could hardly blame them."

"If you and Arthur are running it, I'm certain people will support you." She pressed her head into the side of the chair. "I know I will."

"Seriously? You'd still take supplies from us?"

"Yes. As long as your dad doesn't have anything to do with the place."

"Thank you. That's sweet of you. Are you all set for the grand opening today?"

"I think so." She didn't like to mention that she was waiting to find out if Gordon had poisoned her ice cream. The poor woman had enough to worry about.

"I'm sorry, but I won't be there to support you. I can't show my face at the moment."

"I understand," Lily said. "Don't hide away for too long, though. None of this is your fault."

"Thank you for being so lovely," Sally said. "I hope you have a great turnout today."

"Thanks." Lily told her she'd talk to her soon and ended the call.

She didn't budge from the chair until Ted returned an hour later.

"And?" she asked, letting him into the flat.

"He didn't tamper with any of the food he gave you," Ted said, following her into the kitchen.

"Okay." She wasn't particularly reassured. "Of course he'd say that, though. How do we know he's telling the truth?"

"He admitted to considering it, but apparently Sally had been keen to visit the ice cream shop and he was concerned about her being poisoned."

"So he has his limits?" Lily asked mockingly. "He draws the line at poisoning his own daughter." She leaned against the counter. "I'm still not sure I can trust his word."

"You would if you'd seen the way Sergeant Proctor spoke to him. He really read him the riot act, warning him how much more trouble he'd be in if any children ended up harmed because of him." He wrapped an arm around Lily's shoulders and she slumped against him. "I genuinely don't think there's a problem with the ice cream. You also said you tested it, didn't you?"

"Yeah. I felt fine."

"There we go then. We'll go ahead with the opening."

"I suppose so," Lily mumbled.

"First, you need a nap."

"I don't have time to sleep. I have stuff to do."

"Like what?"

"Like move the ice cream from the freezers into the display case, and write the menu on the blackboard, put out napkins and make sure the place is neat and tidy."

"If you give me your list of flavours for the menu I can do all of that."

Emotions clogged Lily's throat as she shook her head.

"It's not up for discussion," Ted told her. "Go and rest. I'll make sure the place is ready for your first customers."

"I need to call Seren. She was going to come and help…"

"I'll call her. Please just go and lie down."

"Just for half an hour," she agreed. "My brain probably won't slow down enough for me to sleep, anyway. Not with so much to do."

It turned out she was wrong on that front. She was asleep almost as soon as she lay down, and she slept solidly until she felt a gentle pressure on her shoulder.

"Wake up, sleepyhead," a soft voice said.

She blinked a few times until Seren came into focus.

"Sorry to wake you, but we need you downstairs soon."

"What time is it?" Lily asked blearily.

"Quarter to two. You have time for a quick shower."

"Oh, my gosh!" Lily was alert in an instant. "I should have been up ages ago. I have things to do…"

"Ted and I did it. Kit helped too."

"You're amazing. Thank you so much."

"No problem. I heard you stayed at the hospital with Flynn all night." Her eyes flashed with mirth.

"I was worried and didn't want to leave him alone," Lily said, swinging her legs off the bed.

"Are you and he a thing now?"

"No, we're just friends. We talked about our kiss and..." She dragged her fingers through her hair. "We're just friends."

"You don't seem too happy about that."

"It's good," she said. "It's really good."

Seren nodded, apparently content to leave the subject alone for now. "How is he?"

"He seemed okay this morning." Lily grabbed her phone from the bedside table. "I haven't heard anything since then. I guess he's asleep."

"How long does he need to stay in hospital?"

"Just until tomorrow." Lily rubbed at her forehead. "I can't believe I'm opening the shop while he's in hospital. He's helped me so much with getting everything organised. It feels wrong that he's not here."

"It'll be fine." Seren gave her arm a rub. "I also have good news. Glynis is back home. Apparently it might take a while for her to recover completely, but she's feeling much better. She said to tell you she's sorry she can't make it today."

"It's great that's she's back home," Lily said.

Seren nodded. "Now get ready and let's get the party started."

Even after the nap, Lily really wasn't in a party mood.

At least she was thankful to have her friends around her. Hopefully, once she was in the thick of things, she'd be able to relax and enjoy it.

Chapter Thirty Eight

FLYNN SLEPT for longer than he'd intended. His pounding head protested when he forced himself up in the middle of the afternoon. As he struggled to get dressed, his limbs felt as though they'd been filled with lead. Perching on the bed to catch his breath, he had the overwhelming urge to lie down again. If he did, he'd be asleep within moments and he couldn't imagine he'd wake again until the following morning. Which meant he absolutely couldn't lie down.

The door handle clicked and he snapped his gaze to the door. If it was Lily and she'd postponed the opening, he was going to be furious. Or at least mildly annoyed since he wasn't sure he had the energy for more than that.

Sergeant Proctor looked slightly puzzled. "They said you weren't up and about yet. How are you feeling?"

"I've been better, but I'll survive."

"Glad to hear it. You gave us a bit of a scare."

"I'm fine," he said while his eyelids felt as though someone had tied weights to them.

"The doctor says you'll need a week off work."

"I'll probably only need a couple of days."

The sergeant stood up straighter. "You'll take a week, and longer if you need it. No arguing."

Flynn didn't have it in him to argue – he barely managed a shrug. He needed to get up, but gravity seemed to be stronger than usual.

Sergeant Proctor cleared his throat. "I thought I should let you know I called your dad last night. Wanted to keep him abreast of the situation."

"Right," Flynn said. "Thanks." If he had any energy he might be put out that he hadn't had so much as a message from his dad. And he obviously hadn't bothered to let his mum know he was in hospital or his phone wouldn't have stopped.

"I don't know what happened to get you transferred over here," the sergeant said, making Flynn's brow wrinkle at the change of subject.

"Really?" Maybe his brain wasn't functioning properly because he'd have sworn the sergeant knew all about it.

"I heard a version of events," he said, walking over to the window. "I realise now it might not have been the whole story."

Flynn managed a quiet, humourless laugh. "Right. Okay."

"I'd be interested to hear your side of things, if you want to tell it."

He shook his head. "I've been here for almost three months, and now you're asking me what happened?"

"When I spoke to your dad last night—"

Flynn cut him off. "You spoke to my dad and realised that a guy who doesn't care that his son is lying in a hospital bed might not be the great guy that everyone thinks he is." He sucked in a breath. "That's about the size of it, isn't it?"

The sergeant only looked at him sympathetically.

"My dad might not be drowning in paternal affection, but

he's also not a liar. Whatever he told you about me was probably the truth."

"I'm not entirely convinced about that."

"It doesn't matter anyway," Flynn snapped.

"No," Sergeant Proctor replied levelly. "It doesn't. I enjoy working with you. You're good at your job and you're a decent man. That's what matters."

Shocked, Flynn just stared at the sergeant as the words sunk in. "You may be overestimating me," he finally managed through the lump in his throat.

The sergeant chuckled. "I didn't say you don't have your flaws. I can list them, if you want?"

"As lovely as that sounds, I'm just on my way out of here."

"I thought you had to stay another night."

Flynn pushed up from the bed and picked up his bag. "The doctor said I'm fine. I'll just be lethargic for a day or two." Which felt like the understatement of the century, but he really didn't see the need to stay in the hospital another night.

In the hallway, he almost collided with a nurse coming his way.

"You're not supposed to leave today," she said. "Where are you going?"

"I'm fine to leave," he murmured, wishing people would stop making him waste his energy on speaking.

"The doctor won't sign you out until tomorrow morning at the earliest." She looked frantically at the sergeant, who clapped a hand on Flynn's shoulder and almost made him crumple under the weight.

"Stay here another night," he said. "What's the rush to get home?"

"I'm not going home," he said through gritted teeth.

"Lily's opening the ice cream shop today and I promised I'd be there."

"Given the circumstances, I'm sure she'll understand you not being there."

"I know that," he said as he set off along the brightly lit hallway.

He caught the sergeant exchanging words with the nurse, but he didn't care what they said, he was leaving and that was that.

When the sergeant plucked Flynn's bag from his hand, a ripple of irritation expanded his chest. "I really don't have the energy to argue with you, but I am leaving."

"I can see that." The sergeant's eyebrows rose in amusement. "If you can manage to hold a pen, you need to sign a document to say you're leaving against medical advice. And then you need to let me drive you to Lily's place. Those are my terms. You can take them or leave them."

"Okay," he agreed, relieved at the thought of being driven over there. It wasn't far, but he wasn't sure he'd have made it on foot.

As it was, even getting himself into the Land Rover felt like a mammoth task.

"Need a leg up?" the sergeant asked, amused as he held the door for him.

Ignoring the sarge's newfound sense of humour, Flynn hauled himself into the car.

"Are you sure you don't just want to go home?" the sergeant asked when he put the car into gear.

"No." He leaned his head back and battled against sleep. "I promised Lily I'd be there."

"I guess I could eat an ice cream."

"Are you going to stay and babysit me?"

"I don't know about that, but I don't want to miss out on

watching you get shouted out when Lily realises you left the hospital against medical advice."

Flynn smiled at that.

"You two have got pretty close, haven't you?"

"My partner in solving crime," he said, as his eyelids closed.

A couple of minutes later, the car stopped and he blinked his eyes open.

"You're not really supposed to drive on the promenade," he teased.

"I didn't think you'd make it unless I parked right outside the door. I'm still not convinced you'll make it that far."

"I'm all right," he insisted and reached for the handle.

"Hang on," Sergeant Proctor said, making him pause. "There's something I wanted to mention... I know you're only supposed to be here for a limited time, but if you wanted to stay longer, I'd be happy to have you."

That woke Flynn up, though he wasn't sure how to react. "I'll be honest, I didn't think you liked me very much."

"I don't always like the way you go about things," he said. "And I think we see things differently sometimes. But that's not necessarily a bad thing. I meant what I said before – you're a good officer."

"Thanks," Flynn said, slightly uncomfortable with his superior being so sentimental. "I didn't think there was a position for another officer here. I was an add-on, wasn't I?"

"Yes. But there's no harm in asking. If you're interested in staying longer?"

Flynn pressed a hand against his forehead. "I miss London," he said automatically. He missed being busy in his job and the camaraderie with his colleagues. He missed the adrenaline rush of going from one call to another with barely any time to process the situations he was dealing with.

At the same time, he no longer hated being on the Scillies. Not like when he'd first arrived. His eyes flicked to the ice cream shop and the bustle inside.

He didn't hate it at all.

"It's not as though I need an answer now," the sergeant said. "Just let me know if you'd like me to look into it."

"Thanks, Sarge," he said and pulled on the door handle.

Chapter Thirty-Nine

DOLING out ice cream and chatting with customers should have been a pleasant distraction for Lily, but her mind kept wandering to Flynn, lying in a hospital bed. She had to keep reminding herself he was fine. He was safe in the hospital and as soon as she'd finished stuffing people with ice cream she could check on him.

"Why don't you go and mingle?" Ted suggested as he ran the scoop through the cherry ripple chocolate. That was Flynn's favourite and the first batch was almost all gone. After handing the ice cream over to the young woman across the counter, Ted looked at her questioningly. "Did you even hear me?"

She dragged her gaze up to him. "What did you say?"

"Sit down for five minutes. I can manage here."

"It's okay." She smiled weakly. "Thanks again for helping."

"I'm enjoying myself," he told her happily. "You must be pleased with the turnout?"

"I am." There were a surprising number of familiar faces,

too. It seemed she knew more people on the island than she'd realised.

Her first customers had been the couple from the bed-and-breakfast where she'd stayed when she'd first come to the island. Flora and Rodney had been so enthusiastic about the ice cream shop that it had been an instant mood boost for Lily. Their gardener, Oscar, had been in with his girlfriend, too. And there was a gaggle of teenagers hanging around outside, which included Rhys and Jessica, and of course Max and Jory.

There'd also been a constant stream of Trenearys. A bunch of whom now occupied a table at the side of the room, keeping the noise level up, as they always did.

"Seriously, take a break," Ted said. "You look as though you could do with it."

She shook her head, worried that if she stopped and sat down, someone might ask if she was okay, which would be all it would take for her to lose control of her emotions. Keeping busy was her best bet. Another hour or two and things would wind down and she could check on Flynn. She'd feel better when she saw him and was certain he was okay.

Her gaze flicked to the edge of the room, where Dante Accardi stood in silence with his glamorous, dark-haired wife. His focus was on the strawberry cheesecake ice cream, which he was eating slowly from the cone.

Glancing up, he caught her watching him.

"We have a problem," he said, taking a few steps towards her.

Her stomach churned in response to his grave expression. "What?" she asked nervously, certain she wasn't emotionally stable enough to take negative feedback.

"It's good," he said, raising his cone slightly.

"Yeah?" She waited for the *but*. There was definitely going to be a *but*.

"I don't need to teach you anything." He shook his head and took another bite.

"Excuse me?" Lily said, wishing he'd stop talking in riddles.

"I promised to teach you about gelato if you helped me, but you don't need my help. It's not gelato like in Italy, but it's... special."

"Thank you," she said, while her heart settled back to a more regular rhythm.

"You helped me," he said, strolling over to the counter. "You found the person who sabotaged me. How will I repay you?"

She blew out a breath. "Cash would be fine," she said, making Ted chuckle beside her.

Dante waved a hand as though batting the suggestion away. "Come in the restaurant sometime and I'll make you dinner. Free of charge."

"That would be nice."

"Bring your boyfriend," he added.

"I don't have a boyfriend."

"The policeman," Dante said, as though maybe it had just slipped her mind.

"He's not my boyfriend." She didn't have to glance at Ted to know he was grinning.

Dante shrugged. "Bring him anyway."

"Thank you," Lily said. "I'll take you up on that."

"I'll see you soon," he said, reaching for his wife's hand and leading her to the door where Denzel was just walking in.

His eyes did a quick sweep of the room as he walked to the counter. Lily caught his gaze lingering on Mirren for an extra second.

"Hey," Lily said. "How are you?"

"Not too bad." His eyebrows twitched together. "I heard about Gordon and everything."

"Crazy, isn't it?"

"Yeah. I've been with Sally most of the day."

"How's she doing?"

"Hard to say. She's struggling to get her head around it all, but she's resilient. I'm sure she'll be okay."

"I hope so." She glanced at the ice cream selection. "You said you like banana, right?"

"Yeah."

Lily was preparing him a cone of banana and hazelnut when Mirren strode over to join him at the counter. Sneaking an arm around his waist, she leaned in and planted a quick peck on his lips.

"What are you doing?" he asked, glancing nervously over her shoulder.

"It's all right," she whispered. "They know."

Not sure whether it was supposed to be a private conversation, Lily took her time pressing the scoop of ice cream firmly onto the cone.

"What do you mean, they know?" Denzel asked in a panic.

"I told them about us," Mirren said.

"All of them?"

"Yes."

Disbelief flashed in Denzel's eyes.

"It's all right," Mirren said. "It turns out that Trystan and Noah already suspected. Apparently, we weren't as sneaky as we thought – they've seen you coming and going from the house."

Denzel groaned.

"They'd mentioned it to Lowen, so he wasn't surprised either."

"Oh my gosh," Denzel muttered, scrubbing a hand over his face.

"They're fine with it. Jago said he was happy for me."

"And Kit?" Denzel whispered.

"Kit was surprised." Her smile slipped then. "He hasn't said much, but I'm sure he'll be fine once he gets used to the idea."

"Sorry," Lily said, unable to hang back with the ice cream any longer.

Denzel muttered his thanks and she waved him away when he tried to pay.

"I thought you'd be pleased," Mirren said, apparently not concerned about Lily overhearing the conversation. "You wanted me to tell them."

"Yes, but they're all here." His jaw was tight as he glanced over at the Trenearys, who were chatting loudly. "I feel a little blind-sided."

"They are a little intimidating," Lily said, feeling a jolt of sympathy for Denzel.

"My boys?" Mirren said, eyes widening.

"Don't get me wrong," Lily said. "I think they're all lovely, but you have a big family. When they're all together, they can be a bit..." She glanced over at the crowd of them and felt another burst of sympathy for Denzel. "It can be over-whelming to be around all of them," she finished.

"Exactly," Denzel said, then licked at his ice cream when it began to drip down the cone. "Can I just go home?" he asked Mirren sheepishly.

"No." She took his hand and led him away.

Lily wasn't sure if she imagined the hush that fell over the shop as the two of them approached the rest of the Trenearys. It was only momentary, and then the chatting recommenced, and there was some shuffling around as they made space for Denzel.

"What was that all about?" Ted asked, appearing beside Lily.

She smiled. "What did it look like?"

"Mirren and Denzel?" he asked, wide-eyed.

"Yep."

"Wow." Ted stared across the room for a moment. "Good for them," he said after a moment, then smiled at a woman walking up to the counter.

Lily's eyes roamed the ice cream counter. "I'll grab another tub of cherry ripple from the back," she told Ted, who'd already taken over with serving the customer.

Away from the bustle of the shop, her mind strayed to Flynn. A wave of exhaustion had her stopping with her hand on the freezer door. She inhaled deeply and gave herself a mental talking to. She just needed to get through the next couple of hours without falling apart. That was all.

After a few deep breaths, her shoulders relaxed somewhat, but she still felt far too tightly wound.

"Good call on getting Ted to do all the work," a soft voice said.

"You're supposed to be in the hospital," she snapped as she swung around. Her breath hitched at the sight of Flynn looking dishevelled and deathly pale.

"I figured a trip to the ice cream shop wouldn't kill me."

"Maybe not, but I might." She crossed the room and tilted her head. "You look like death. What on earth possessed you to leave the hospital?"

"I promised you moral support. And you know I don't like to miss out on your little adventures."

"Do you feel as bad as you look?" she asked.

He shrugged and his solemn gaze bored into her. "Do *you?*"

"I'm fine," she insisted, but tears filled her eyes.

Flynn's arms wrapped around her and she sank into his embrace. With her face nestled against his neck, she inhaled the scent of him and felt her tense muscles relax.

"I was so bloody worried about you," she mumbled against his skin.

He kissed the top of her head. "It was only a scratch."

Stepping back, she wiped stray tears from the corners of her eyes. "You look as though you might be about to pass out."

"It's a definite possibility. The doctor really wasn't joking about the lethargy. I feel as though I could sleep for a week."

She touched his cheek and looked at him sternly. "You are such a pain in the bum sometimes. I'm opening a shop today and you want me to play nursemaid too?"

"Moral support," he whispered, then swayed as though he might seriously be about to collapse.

Lily kept a hold of his arm but stepped towards the doorway and scanned the crowd of Trenearys before calling out to Jago.

His head whipped in her direction and she beckoned him with a flick of her hand.

"What have I done?" he asked, grimacing as he walked into the back room.

"Nothing."

"Why are you scowling at me, then?"

"My scowl is directed at this idiot." She moved closer to Flynn, who was definitely swaying.

Jago smiled. "I thought you were still in the hospital."

"I got bored," Flynn told him.

"Can you do me a favour and help him upstairs?" she asked.

"I'm fine," Flynn argued, but stumbled when he took a step. Jago moved quickly and took hold of his arm.

"Put him in my bed," Lily said. "He's not supposed to be up and about."

"I can manage to get upstairs," Flynn said, but looked dubiously at the staircase in the corner.

"Do you know how annoyed I'll be if you collapsed and fall down the stairs while I have a shop full of people to deal with?" Lily resumed scowling at him. "Just let Jago help you."

"Fine, but I'll only sleep for an hour, then I'll come and help you."

"Sure you will," Lily said while Jago ushered him towards the stairs.

A smile pulled at Lily's lips as she watched them go.

At the top of the stairs, Jago said something Lily couldn't make out, but whatever it was made Flynn laugh. The sound made Lily's stomach flutter with butterflies.

He's going to leave in a few months, she reminded herself, but knew that there was nothing she could do to keep from getting too attached.

She was certain she was already doomed to get her heart broken by PC Flynn Grainger.

"Lily!" Seren called, snapping her from her trance. "Are you okay?"

"I'm fine," she said, smiling as she turned to her friend.

Doomed, but fine.

Chapter Forty

PREDICTABLY, Flynn didn't reappear to help Lily in the shop. She hadn't for one moment expected him to, and she was actually glad he hadn't. As things quietened down, she nipped up to check on him, relieved to see him sleeping soundly.

He was still in a peaceful slumber when she trudged upstairs once the shop was closed and everything tidied up. After getting changed into her pyjamas, she had a momentary hesitation over whether to sleep on the couch before deciding against it. Flynn finally stirred when she slipped into bed beside him.

"Did I miss it?" he asked, then yawned widely.

"You missed it."

His forehead wrinkled. "Sorry."

"It doesn't matter."

"It matters to me," he said, shifting onto his side. "Because now Ted will forever get all the credit for helping you."

A smile pulled at the corners of her mouth. "Ted was very helpful. As were Kit and Seren. I really found out who my true friends were today. Some really went above and beyond...

and some people just slept the whole day…" Her words turned into laughter as Flynn dug his fingers under her ribs.

"How did it go?" he asked seriously.

"I think it went well. Lots of people came, and everyone seemed to love the ice cream. As long as no one gets ill, I'll call it a success."

"No one will get ill. You tested all the ice cream yourself. I still think you're crazy for doing that."

"Ted and Sergeant Proctor also questioned Gordon about it and he swore he hadn't tampered with the ingredients for the ice cream, but he's hardly the most trustworthy person."

Flynn sighed heavily and sank further into the pillow. "I can't believe it was him. Why would he do that?"

Lily told him about her conversation with Sally, and they spent an hour chewing over all the details of the case.

When they'd finally exhausted rehashing it all, Flynn looked at her wearily. "Would you mind if I sleep here tonight? I don't think I can face walking home."

"It's fine. I assumed you would."

"I can move to the couch," he said without enthusiasm.

"You can also just sleep there. Whatever you want."

"It's comfy here," he said. "If you're sure you don't mind."

"I don't. Are you hungry? I can make you a sandwich or something."

He gave a small shake of the head. "I'm not hungry."

"That's got to be a first," she joked.

This time, when he reached out to tickle her, his fingers hit the exposed skin between her vest and her pyjama trousers and sent goosebumps rippling over her skin. She batted him away with a smile and a gentle admonishment.

After turning out the lamp, she sank back into her pillow, tired but entirely content.

"I should probably call my mum," Flynn said while they ate a full English breakfast in Lily's small kitchen the following morning.

"Does she know you were in hospital?" Lily asked, spearing a piece of bacon and dabbing it into the yolk of her fried egg.

"Apparently not."

"What does that mean?"

He bit into a slice of toast. "She'd have called me about a hundred times by now if she knew. Not that it matters. It's probably better she didn't know."

"How come you seem annoyed?" Lily asked. "What am I missing?"

His shoulders shifted in a nonchalant shrug. "My dad knew I was in hospital, but he clearly didn't think it was worth informing my mum."

"Has your dad been in touch?"

"Nope." A muscle in his jaw twitched and he kept his gaze fixed on his food.

"That's a bit weird, isn't it?"

She thought back to the way Sergeant Proctor had looked when she'd asked if he knew Flynn as a child, and wondered if there was more to Flynn's relationship with his dad than he let on. He'd mentioned that his mum had essentially raised him as a single parent and he'd only seen his dad sporadically growing up, but she didn't know much more than that. She'd assumed there was some sort of connection, given that his dad was also a police officer.

"I'd probably have been more surprised if he had called." He rubbed at his forehead with the back of his hand. "You'd think I'd be used to him by now and it wouldn't bother me."

"But it does?"

"He's my dad," he said, then took a deep breath and tucked into his breakfast again. "I forgot to tell you, I had an interesting conversation with the sergeant yesterday."

"What about?"

His smile slipped and a flash of uncertainty hit his eyes and was gone again in an instant. "He told me I'm a good officer and he likes working with me."

"That's high praise." Lily smirked. "Are we certain someone didn't poison the sergeant? It sounds as though he was confused."

"Shut up," he said, giving her a playful kick under the table.

He loaded the last of his bacon and egg onto his fork and polished off his meal in one huge mouthful. His gaze was on the pin board hanging beside the table when he washed it all down with a swig of coffee. "Now that you've solved the mystery of the poisonings, we should get back to figuring out the other mystery." Reaching out, he unpinned the picture of the cafe owner and set it between them.

"I told you, I think I want to leave it be. Besides, we've had no luck in finding her so far."

"Don't be so defeatist. I really think we'll find her, eventually."

Lily set her cutlery on the plate and let out a long sigh as she picked up the photo. "I wish I had your confidence." Her eyes snagged on something at the bottom of the photo and she shifted her grasp of it slightly as her heart rate went haywire.

"What's wrong?" Flynn asked.

She forgot to breathe as she shifted her thumb to partially cover the object at the bottom of the picture.

"Lily?" Flynn said.

"It's not a crucifix," she muttered, more to herself than Flynn.

"What isn't?"

"The necklace... I thought it was a cross, but it's an anchor."

Flynn moved beside her to look at the photo. "It's clearly an anchor."

"Yes. In the picture it is..." She looked at him in a panic. "But I've seen it in real life... Or I think I have." Feeling suddenly stupid, she shook her head. "No. That can't be right. She wouldn't still be wearing the same necklace, would she?"

"She might," Flynn said. "Where did you see it?"

"The owner is called Gail," Lily said, thinking aloud. "It can't be her."

"*Who?*" Flynn growled.

Lily's pulse raced, and she thought of the day she'd been at Glynis's house and the way Maria had been so adamant that someone was out to get them.

"She meant me and her," she muttered, knowing she was rambling but unable to stop herself. "She thought someone was out to get us. And if she's using a different name, that could explain why she got so stressed about the papers on the table. Maybe because it had her real name on it. And if the necklace is an anchor it explains why she was so confused when I asked if she was religious..."

Lily fell silent and looked at Flynn, who'd returned to the seat opposite her. His patient gaze made her shake her head in an attempt to straighten her jumbled thoughts.

"Sorry," she said.

"Who do you think it is?"

"Maria." She closed her eyes as she let everything sink in. "I think Maria owns the ice cream shop."

"The woman who lives with Glynis?"

Lily gave a curt nod. When she finally opened her eyes again, she expected Flynn to ask if she was sure. He didn't speak at all though, just looked at her in that way he did when she was investigating something. He trusted her judgement without questioning it.

"Maria moved to the island not long before I did," Lily said, trying to fit all the pieces of the puzzle together. "And Glynis said they were old friends. Maybe from when Maria – or Gail, if that's who she really is – lived here before. It also explains why she's been keeping such a low profile and not going out much." Her eyes flicked to Flynn. "Do you think Glynis knows? Has she been coming into the shop to spy on me and report back to Maria?"

"I don't know," Flynn said. "I wouldn't rule it out."

Lily pushed her fingers into her temples. "Maybe I'm wrong," she said frantically. "I could be way off the mark."

"Maybe," Flynn said. "But I don't think it will be difficult to find out."

Lily nodded slowly.

"What were you saying about someone being out to get you?" he asked with a deep frown.

"When I visited Maria and she was ill, I don't think she knew anyone else had received the welcome baskets. I think she had it in her head that it was only me and her who'd been targeted. At the time, I thought she was delirious from a fever or something..." She inhaled deeply as she thought back on Maria's ramblings. "She thought someone was trying to kill us."

"Why would she think that?"

"Good question." Lily paused. "But we know there was a fire at the ice cream shop, around the same time that my parents died in a fire."

"You're thinking that might not be a coincidence..."

She shrugged. "Maybe that's what Maria was worried about... that whoever started the fires is still out to get us." Looking at Flynn's bemused features, she slapped a hand over her mouth. "I sound crazy, don't I?"

"No," he said unconvincingly.

With her mind reeling, she looked bleakly at Flynn. "I keep wondering..." She trailed off, not sure she really wanted to voice what was on her mind.

"What?" Flynn coaxed.

"When I think about my childhood, I have this horrible feeling that maybe I grew up on the run." She laughed at the absurdity of the words and dropped her head to her hands. "I realise exactly how this sounds, but when I look back, it kind of makes sense. The way we moved around so much and the way my uncle was always talking about needing to be prepared for anything. When he died, I found stuff at his house that didn't make sense..."

"Such as?" Flynn asked.

She opened her mouth, then closed it again, feeling as though she'd said too much. "Such as the photo of the ice cream shop," she said eventually. "He'd convinced me that my memories of it weren't real."

Sighing, she covered her face with her hands. After a moment, Flynn peeled her hands away and held them in his.

"We're going to figure this out," he told her plainly. "We'll talk to Maria and get you your answers. I promise."

Lily nodded, feeling as close to finding out the truth as she'd ever been.

She just wasn't convinced she was going to like what she found.

To be continued ...

A note from the author...

Dear reader,

Thanks so much for reading A Poisonous Plot. Hopefully you enjoyed Lily and Flynn's latest antics.

For those of you wondering about the mysterious Thorned Sleeping Beauty plant, I thought I should mention that it is purely a figment of my imagination. No such plant exists.

While doing my research I found a lot of plants which would make you mildly ill and some which can kill very quickly. I wanted something which was overall pretty harmless, and I also wanted to add a bit of blood and drama! So I decided to use artistic license and I made up something to fit the story.

I hope you enjoyed it!

Don't miss the next book in the series...

Dead in the Water

(Lily Larkin Mysteries: book 4)

A body in the harbour. A yacht full of secrets. And a race against the tide to find the truth.

With her ice cream shop thriving, Lily feels at home in the close-knit Isles of Scilly. And now that she's uncovered the shop's true owner, she hopes the long-held mysteries of her unconventional childhood will soon be solved.

But when her friendship with the charming PC Grainger hits troubled waters, she has little time to dwell—especially after a customer is found floating lifeless in the harbour.

Determined to uncover the truth, Lily turns her attention to the victim's travel companions—longtime friends and co-owners of a luxury motor yacht. But the closer she gets, the more secrets she unearths.

Was the death truly an accident, or is there something more sinister at play?

With the suspects preparing to sail away and her trusted ally absent from her side, Lily must decide—can she crack the case alone, or will she set aside her pride and seek PC Grainger's help before the killer leaves with the tide?

Also by Hannah Ellis

The Lily Larkin Series

Death on the Rocks (Book 1)

Malicious Intent (Book 2)

A Poisonous Plot (Book 3)

Dead in the Water (Book 4)

The Isles of Scilly Series

The Weekend Getaway (Book 1)

A Change of Heart (Book 2)

The Summer Escape (Book 3)

The Potter's House (Book 4)

An Unexpected Guest (Book 5)

The Hope Cove Series

The Cottage at Hope Cove (Book 1)

Escape to Oakbrook Farm (Book 2)

Summer at The Old Boathouse (Book 3)

Whispers at the Bluebell Inn (Book 4)

The House on Lavender Lane (Book 5)

The Bookshop of Hopes and Dreams (Book 6)

Winter Wishes in Hope Cove (Book 7)

There's Something about Scarlett (Book 8)

The Single Dads Club Series

It Takes a Village (Book 1)

Riding the Waves (Book 2)

Playing for Keeps (Book 3)

Rules of Engagement (Book 4)

The Loch Lannick Series

Coming Home to the Loch (Book 1)

The Castle by the Loch (Book 2)

Fireworks over the Loch (Book 3)

The Cafe at the Loch (Book 4)

Secrets at the Loch (Book 5)

Surprises at the Loch (Book 6)

Finding Hope at the Loch (Book 7)

Fragile Hearts by the Loch (Book 8)

New Arrivals at the Loch (Book 9)

The Lucy Mitchell Series

Beyond the Lens (Book 1)

Beneath These Stars (Book 2)

Always With You (Standalone novel)

The Friends Like These Series

Friends Like These (Book 1)

Christmas with Friends (Book 2)

My Kind of Perfect (Book 3)

A Friend in Need (Book 4)

All of Hannah's books can be found here:

http://Author.to/HannahEllis

Hannah has also written a series of children's books aimed at 5-9 year olds under the pen name, Hannah Sparks. You can find the first book in that series here: https://mybook.to/WhereDragonsFly

About the Author

When she's not writing, Hannah enjoys spending time with her husband and kids. She loves to read, do jigsaw puzzles and go for long walks. She also enjoys yoga and drinks a lot of tea!

Hannah can be found online at the following places:

Facebook: @authorhannahellis

Instagram: @authorhannahellis

Website: www.authorhannahellis.com

If you'd like to be kept up to date with news about Hannah's books you can sign up to receive emails from her through her website:

www.authorhannahellis.com/newsletter

Printed in Great Britain
by Amazon

59607660R00162